"YOU'VE HEARD MY TALE, LORI, AND NOW I WILL exact my price for it," Noble said.

He watched as she nervously wet her lips, which whetted his appetite to consume them in a fury. He swept aside their coffee cups and gripped the lapel of her robe. A small jerk, and he began to trace her lips with his tongue.

"My kiss, Lori. I would have that kiss from you now."

"Oh . . . okay," she stammered. "But just a kiss. That's all."

Noble laughed softly. "Could it be you have as much to learn from me as I have from you?"

"No doubt," she agreed, her breath coming shallow and fast. "But what does that have to do with a kiss?"

"Only everything, my dear." He nipped at her bottom lip. "I've yet to truly kiss you. But once I do, you'll realize that any real kiss from me will never be *just a kiss.*" Then he pressed her down to the table and claimed her. . . .

WHAT ARE *LOVESWEPT* ROMANCES?

They are stories of true romance and touching emotion. We believe those two very important ingredients are constants in our highly sensual and very believable stories in the LOVESWEPT line. Our goal is to give you, the reader, stories of consistently high quality that may sometimes make you laugh, sometimes make you cry, but are always fresh and creative and contain many delightful surprises within their pages.

Most romance fans read an enormous number of books. Those they truly love, they keep. Others may be traded with friends and soon forgotten. We hope that each LOVESWEPT romance will be a treasure—a "keeper." We will always try to publish

LOVE STORIES YOU'LL NEVER FORGET
BY AUTHORS YOU'LL ALWAYS REMEMBER

The Editors

Loveswept 730

PISTOL
IN HIS
POCKET

OLIVIA M.
RUPPRECHT

BANTAM BOOKS
NEW YORK · TORONTO · LONDON · SYDNEY · AUCKLAND

PISTOL IN HIS POCKET
A Bantam Book / March 1995

Love and gratitude to Trayce Primm,
my fellow wordweaver whose
auspicious talent is eclipsed only
by the depth of her friendship.
You were right, Trayce,
progress is not a linear path;
faith and ability *are* facets
of the same stone.

Also, many thanks to Chris Bock,
for sharing his expertise with such
enthusiasm that I can almost
understand why someone would
actually want to climb
an icy mountain or the brutal
beauty of a mile-high rock.

PROLOGUE

Juneau, Alaska—1898

WANTED
LUKE LASSITER
FOR ARMED ROBBERY AND MURDER
$5000 REWARD
DEAD OR ALIVE

Leaning forward for a better view of the outlaw's roughly sketched face, the rider felt his great stallion prance beneath him as icy raindrops pelted his cheeks.

A soft chuckle passed the hard lips clamping a cheroot, red tip glowing in the moon's pale light. Cigar smoke blended with the white puffs of his breath. In a precise, cultured voice, the rider said, "So tell me, Bitter, do you think the picture does me justice?" At the word *justice*, the horse's snort coincided with the man's low snarl.

"Nor do I," he agreed, neatly ripping the paper

from the post to which it was tacked then stuffing it beneath his fur-lined coat. "A memento, Bitter. After tonight, my days of disguise will soon be ended. Ah well, fond as I have become of playing Lucky Luke, there will be no need for him once Noble Zhivago has back what is rightfully his."

Even as he said it Noble knew that unless the dead could be resurrected, he would never have back all that was rightfully his. He felt his hatred surge high and bright, his thirst for vengeance begging to be quenched.

He threw down the cheroot, checked his pistol, then urged Bitter into a lazy saunter. Hat tipped down, Noble nodded to the few stragglers he passed on the main street. It seemed the remaining populace of Juneau had the good sense to favor a fire within over the brewing storm outside.

Such piteous creature comforts, he thought, while images of England played their seductively sweet refrain in his memory. How he missed the simple pleasure of taking tea in an elegant drawing room. And ah, but to bow over the gloved hand of a gentle-born lady, to spend an evening in the company of notorious actors after indulging his frivolous affection for high drama with a Shakespearean play. And a true court of law— now there was real drama, moving soliloquies to make, or to destroy savagely with an eloquent rebuttal.

Noble sighed deeply. If not for the grinding need to see justice done, he would still be living in his mother's beloved England and enjoying the life he'd taken refuge in for nearly two decades before returning to the place of his youth. Here, in Juneau, he had been driven for five years by his vengeful mission: retribution for his parents' deaths, the reclaiming of their land and the gold stripped from it.

Even among relatives in England, even with the comfort of leather-bound books and stately grounds, he had not forgotten that mission—one that had determined his current existence.

He lived, if he could call it living, in nearby Skagway, where he drew up legal claims for prospectors and defended this drunken murderer or that claim-jumping bastard as best he could amid vigilante law.

Skagway was a deplorable little city, brimming with tents and gold dust and shattered dreams.

But it was perfect for his purposes. In Skagway he could live openly as a respectable citizen while seventy miles south his criminal charges mounted.

His coup de grâce a robbery and murder away, Noble took stock of his surroundings. Compared with Skagway, Juneau seemed a veritable mecca of sophistication.

Oh yes, how very civilized it was. With distaste, he scanned the street and saw that all appeared to be quite normal. Horses whinnied from the posts to which they were tethered. Rowdy shouts and the off-key pound of a piano spilled from the saloon.

He cut his gaze to the bordello and shook his head. Women were in short supply, and those available were usually shared. Even more than a horse-drawn carriage on a cobblestone street, he missed the fairer sex—the sort that didn't paint their faces and allowed a kiss only if a man had won it with charm or worthy intentions.

But enough of this self-indulgent sentimentality. He had a bank to rob and one remaining henchman to kill before the score was settled. It was a Pyrrhic victory at best, but he'd take it, revel in it, and buy back his rightful holdings with the stolen gold that had first been stolen from him. Once he'd seen to that, he'd take a much-needed holiday in England. Attu, his boyhood companion and trusted partner in crime, would be quite happy to watch over the ten thousand acres of Zhivago land, now bled dry of its gold, in his absence.

Ambling past the brightly lit jail, Noble guided Bitter around the dark bank, the last graceless building on the street.

Once in the deserted alley, he secured his black bandanna over his nose and mouth and rode to the bank's rear entry. There, he whispered a promise of oats and sugar, then slid off his trusty steed. From the saddlebag Noble withdrew the clever tools he'd had an ironsmith fashion for him. They weren't as efficient as dynamite but made considerably less noise.

He seemed to have acquired a certain proficiency at this lowly skill of breaking and entering, given his easy dismantling of the knob and the guts of a new lock. As if they were a child's tooth a yank away from coming out, he removed them, then glided a slender, curved bar inside.

His lips tightened as he probed for the metal bolt and found the interior guard missing.

Suspicion and instinct demanded he leave at once. Reason suggested it was simply a matter of human error, albeit a case of gross neglect worthy of immediate dismissal.

Noble swiftly debated. If he left now, it would be a month, perhaps more, before he could schedule another illicit rendezvous with the bank. By then, winter would be settled in deep and Mendenhall Glacier would be even more difficult to traverse. Indeed, he'd likely have to wait until spring before completing his current task.

Shutting out the sharp whisper of instinctive warning, Noble tossed aside the tool and readied his gun. He gave a hard kick to the door. It opened easily and he jumped back at the telltale sound of several clicks in the dark bank.

He saw the flare of the first bullet leaving its chamber, smelled the acrid scent of gunpowder filling the clean air, heard the rapid pound of his heart echo in his ears as he raced against the odds and slung himself astride Bitter.

More bullets than he could count whistled over his head, rushed past his shoulders as Bitter streaked down the alley. The thunder of his hooves beat in time with the slashing pellets of rain, which turned to hail as they approached the icy mountains. Noble calculated a five-minute lead.

A generous calculation. The posse's horses were fresh, and Bitter had endured a three-day trek with only minimal rest. By the time they reached Mendenhall Glacier, the sound of frustrated curses and horses' hooves was increasing alarmingly.

Noble reined in for a few precious seconds.

Take the safest route? But if he did that, they would

be overtaken in short measure. Besides, Skagway was quite possibly no longer a haven, his anonymity no longer assured. Somehow he had been found out; otherwise there would not have been a trap for him.

God be with me. Let the damn bastards have enough sense not to follow.

Once past Mendenhall Glacier's icy expanse, Noble urged Bitter onto a rough mountain trail. A cave, if only they could find a cave, they might make it. As they wound their way up the tortuous path, hail and sleet beat at them.

Suddenly Noble spied a refuge, a yawning shadow unlit by the light of the moon. What mercy to find it, and none too soon. The low curses trailing him were a blatant warning. He had been followed.

His only comfort was the certainty that the posse was now fewer in number, those prizing their lives not daring the risk he had taken. And the trail was narrow— they couldn't converge on him en masse, giving him an advantage.

He could pick them off.

"Bitter," Noble whispered as he unmounted on the ledge's slick lip, "for this night, I'll put you to stud with the finest fillies in all of Alaska. I'll find you once I've taken care of this nasty business. Off with you now—"

A bullet ricocheted off the rock jutting just over his head. And then another and another followed as Noble threw himself against the protective guard of the crevasse. It proved much shallower than he'd thought. Were they simply idiots, or were they absolutely insane? A low rumble high overhead filled the air and still the bullets came. Worse than insane, his pursuers must be suicidal! And why wasn't Bitter taking flight as fast as he could?

His heart lurching, Noble saw his beloved mount rare up, blood spewing from his flanks. And then the horse was plummeting over the ledge like Pegasus stripped of his wings, pawing blindly as he descended into a black abyss.

The bastards, the bloody damn bastards. He'd kill them for what they'd done to Bitter as well as his parents. Heedless of the rumble, now sounding closer to thunder, Noble returned their fire. They were all about to die. What could only be an avalanche was sure to bury each and every one of them alive. But he'd do murder for murder first—

And then white, everything white, silenced his next breath before he could draw it. The heavy pall of snow was freezing. And yet it felt warmer than a stack of wool blankets piled on his body, his mind.

Vaguely, Noble wondered why people wore black to mourn the dead. White, pristine white, seemed far more appropriate. It was the color of purity, of sweet-scented flowers that honored weddings, the christening of innocent babes.

So, too, it honored the deceased, among which he was surely counted. His last coherent thought was more a prayer:

God grant me the peace in death that life has denied me.

ONE

Despite the thin, cold air, sweat beaded Lori Morgan's brow as she dug in the crampons attached to her boots and hoisted herself onto a ledge of rock.

Crouched there, panting, she called up to her climbing partner. "Ryan, gotta rest."

"Wimp," he taunted, his subdued voice echoing from his higher position.

In an effort to work out the stiffness she had acquired on the ascent, Lori flexed her gloved fingers. Lord, she must be a masochist, she decided. Why else would an otherwise sane thirty-year-old woman subject herself to the rigors of climbing for the thrill of a gorgeous view, shared with a bully like Ryan, who didn't have the decency to work up half the sweat she did on their climbs or, for that matter, in the emergency room. Not only that, he made lousy coffee.

At the moment even a cup of Ryan's brew sounded like heaven. Heaven. They should be there any minute.

Unbidden, tears filled her eyes as Mick's image came into her mind, and she wiped them away impatiently. What was the matter with her, still crying with no more than the thought of him three years after a bullet had taken his life? As for herself, it was a wonder she hadn't died of a broken heart. Then again, maybe she'd simply die of exhaustion in the pursuit of this self-punishing pleasure.

"Lori," Ryan called down, "you okay?"

"I'm fine, dammit," she lied. With renewed energy, she repositioned her gear, then struck an ice ax against the challenge she would conquer.

The snow fell from where she'd landed her frustrated blow. "Oh my God," Lori whispered, and began to brush away the snow in earnest. Fascinated, horrified by the sight revealed, she forgot the ever-present need not to disrupt nature and cried out, "Ryan, get down here! *Fast.*"

"Are you in trouble?" he urgently asked.

"No. But hurry. Please, just hurry." Her heart beating so loud she wasn't sure if it was echoing in her head or bouncing off the crevasse, Lori stared at the man she had nearly axed in the face. He was miraculously intact, surely dead, and given the period of his dress, the antique gun poised in his hand, he'd been frozen in time a century ago.

Had he been a prospector searching for gold in the caves? Or had he been an outlaw hiding the gold he'd stolen? Those were wild and woolly days in Alaska, and whoever he was, she was sure he'd have some incredible stories to tell.

Such a shame he'd met his end so young.

Like Mick. Lori pushed away the thought and focused on the man who was held suspended beneath several inches of ice.

He looked like a cross between the original Marlboro man and Clint Eastwood shooting it out in a spaghetti western. There wasn't a woman alive who wouldn't turn her head and change the direction of her walk to get another glimpse of this rough-hewn hunk.

She was still staring at him, mesmerized, when Ryan gained his footing beside her.

"What's the deal?"

"This." Lori tapped at the ice that separated her finger from an aristocratic nose. "Can you believe it?"

"Holy . . . ! It's Encino Man!"

"Yeah. Only he's packing a pistol and looks a lot more civilized than savage." But that wasn't entirely true. He did have something of a savage look about him, tempered by an unmistakable refinement in his chiseled features. "Poor guy," she said, feeling a swift compassion. "Buried alive. What an awful way to go."

"We see a lot worse in the ER. My guess is, he probably didn't have time to draw a last breath, much less suffer."

But he had suffered, if not in death, then in life. Lori shook her head, wondering where in the world the certainty of that thought had come from. She dismissed it. Hell, everyone suffered in life; Lord knew that she'd pulled double duty herself. Even so, she hoped this man had been spared pain.

"What are we going to do with him?" she asked,

puzzled at the sense of ownership and responsibility she felt.

"Want to throw a thermos of my coffee on his face and see if that thaws him out?"

"Acid would be more kind." She tapped her foot, thinking. And touched what felt like the protrusion of a shoe. Kicking at the rounded hardness, she uncovered a boot. "Look! His feet are barely iced over!"

"Great boots. Chisel 'em out and you can borrow them for the next time we go to the Kick and Kaboodle Club."

At her sharp glance, Ryan relented. "Okay, so my jokes are as bad as my coffee. Here's what we do—we get back to the Jeep and contact the authorities. There's got to be some scientists around who'd want to inspect our find."

My find, Lori silently amended.

"I don't like that idea," she said firmly.

"Got a better one? It's the logical thing to do."

Logical, true. But there was something very illogical going on in her head that had her gripping Ryan's arm. "You know what'll happen? They'll say thanks, carve him out, then dissect him in a lab. The *National Enquirer* won't waste a second to make a mint off sneak photos and . . ." She shuddered. How amazingly alive this beautiful man looked, and yet he would be taken apart, gawked at in checkout stands.

"And *what*? For Christ's sake, Lori, he's dead. What do you want to do? Keep him for yourself?" At her look of serious contemplation, Ryan snorted in disbelief.

"Aw, no way. You've gotta be nuts to even think about it."

He was right, she knew that. But there was such dignity and character etched in the man's face that it stirred something inside her. Something that was protective and fierce and urgent and made absolutely no sense at all. She worried her bottom lip, trying to come up with a rational explanation for the irrational direction of her response.

"You know, Ryan, I saw an Oprah show not long ago and she had these people there that planned to be frozen once they died. And there were experts on the subject, too, and they were saying how it was possible to bring people back to life, only the technology hadn't been perfected yet. But they had frozen a dog and revived it and—"

"Lori, get a grip! Cryonics is out there—waaay out there. You're talking sci-fi stuff."

"Maybe," she admitted. "Maybe not. After all, that's what people once thought about electricity, television, putting a man on the moon." She shot him a challenging glance. "Of course, as Einstein once said, 'Great spirits have always encountered violent opposition from mediocre minds.'"

He stared at her, incredulous. "I don't believe it. You're actually serious about this."

Breathless, she answered, "I can't believe it either, because I really think that I am." She pressed her palm to the ice, touching, almost touching what promised to be a broad, masculine chest. She felt a small lurch, a soft flutter in her own. It was a strange sensation, an echo of the moment when the man who would be her husband tapped on the window of her car to issue a citation and ended up waving two tickets to the policeman's ball.

Never would she forget that lilting sensation. Never would she forget the tragedy of its loss. She had lost Mick; maybe that was why she had such a foolish need to try saving this surely unsavable man.

"Look, Lori, we've been friends for a long time. And you know that there's nothing I wouldn't do for you. But—"

"Ditto, Ryan. And that's why I know that I can count on you to keep a lid on this thing and help me figure out how we're going to get him from here to my place. Say next weekend? Don't try to squirm out of it, I know your schedule. We've both got next Saturday free."

Ryan quit grinding his teeth long enough to blow out an exasperated sigh. "Okay, have it way, but just tell me one thing first. What the hell are you going to do with this frozen dude once he thaws out?"

Since she hadn't thought that far ahead, she figured it out as she went. "Before that happens, I'm going to the library and get everything I can find on cryonics. And then there's Dr. Rashid at the hospital—"

"He's a horny lech."

"So what? That horny lech is doing research on low-temperature whatever-he-calls-it for organ preservation. I'll buy him lunch and pick his brain. After that, only two things can happen. If by some miracle our friend here can be resuscitated, I'm a nurse and he's in good hands. If not . . ." *I'll see that he gets a decent burial to make up for the one he didn't get.*

It was more than Mick had gotten. His funeral had resembled a three-ring circus, the grieving widow's picture splashed on the front page of the newspaper. It had not been right. Then again, nursing her wounds at the expense of denying science a look-see wouldn't be right either.

"If he's a goner, I'll turn him over to Dr. Rashid, who can call in his cronies before the anthropologists and the yellow journalists and God only knows who else has at him. Fair enough?"

Ryan hesitated, shook his head, then gave a curt nod. "Jeez, I must be as crazy as you. You want him, you've got him. But we're going to need some help."

"Make that some help who can keep their mouths shut."

"Right. And that definitely reduces the pickings. As it is, there's only three who come to mind."

"Warren, Jacob, and Jennifer." Not only were they top-notch climbers, Warren and Jacob had muscle to spare. As for Jennifer, she had the moxie to keep them both in line and polish her nails while she was at it.

Ryan pulled at his chin. "Once we hack him out, getting him to the bottom won't be easy. He doesn't look light, even minus the ice, but put 'em together and we've got a mother lode of weight to haul."

Lori had to agree. "We could use a stretcher and risk the trail. It's probably the way he came up."

"The trail's too rough, and even if it wasn't, it'd take forever to push him down. Too dangerous. Forget it."

That idea nixed, she searched for another. And came up with one that could land both her and Ryan in big trouble.

"Oh, Ryan," she singsonged. "Guess what I'm thinking."

"I know what you're thinking. Lord, to think like you, I must need my head examined."

She smacked his cheek with a kiss. "I love ya, big guy. I can always count on you to be there for me, no matter what."

"Know what? I hate it when you get sappy." As he spoke they prepared to rappel like marionette birds on sturdy strings. Poised on the ledge, Ryan asked, "Ready?"

"Not quite." No, she wasn't ready. But she wasn't about to tell Ryan that she didn't want to leave the man frozen in time. "First, I want you to tell me what keeps us together."

"What else? It's your addiction to my coffee."

"Get outta here!" She gave him a playful shove and he laughed as he sailed out and down.

Lori took a last, lingering look at the man she felt an unexplainable affinity with. Regretfully she left him, assuring herself that he hadn't moved since before her great-grandmother was born, and surely he wasn't going anywhere before she came back to reclaim him.

As it turned out, they made two trips before exhuming the man from his frozen crypt. The mission was exhausting, exhilarating, a great adventure. One that,

Lori guessed, would enrage the scientific community. What she didn't have to guess about was that she and Ryan would be out of a job if the hospital ever discovered that the emergency helicopter had played an important role in their master plan.

Their last partner in crime was Skip, the pilot, who also took an oath of silence. They couldn't have done it without him and the chopper.

A whoop of jubilation went up from Lori and Jennifer once the icy weight was deposited in the back of Warren's monster truck. Lori blew kisses to Skip, who departed with an enthusiastic thumbs-up signal.

As they waited for the others to return, Lori covered the bulk with a length of heavy canvas, stroked it with a protective caress.

"Now I can breathe again," she said, sighing her relief.

"The question is, will *he* breathe again?" Jennifer gave the canvas a neat slap, which Lori didn't much care for.

"Not likely," she admitted. "The big problem seems to be that when the body's fluids freeze, ice crystals form and damage the cell tissue. There is a chance, though, a really, really slim chance, that if he was frozen almost immediately, the ice crystals wouldn't have had time to form."

"Hey, I'm impressed. Sounds like you know your stuff."

Lori snorted at that. "Don't I wish." If she never read another article on cryogenics, it would be too soon. Despite her BSRN degree, the technical mumbo jumbo supporting the theory that life could be held suspended by totally mind-boggling means had been daunting. As for the phone call she'd made to the cryonics organization, she'd felt like a fledgling Trekkie talking to Star-fleet Command.

But then there was Dr. Rashid, who had been flattered that she had taken an interest in his research. So flattered, in fact, that he'd asked her out twice so they could pick up their lunchtime conversations over dinner.

Dire as her need was to learn as much as she could, she'd turned him down both times. The jerk was married.

"I wonder if he's married," she mused, eyeing the canvas.

"If he was, he sure ain't now," Jennifer pointed out. She cocked an eyebrow. "Know what, Lori? You seem to be a lot more interested in this guy than in any of the others who've been trying to make time with you since . . . well, you know."

It was true, but Lori wasn't about to admit to her romantic fantasies involving the "amazing human Popsicle" as her friends had dubbed him.

With a mischievous smile, Lori said, "Actually, Jenn, if you think about it, he's got some great points in his favor."

"And just what might those be?"

"For one thing, he's harmless, and that's a lot more than I can say for some of the studs who hit on us at the Kick and Kaboodle. The only line dancing they're after is the horizontal two-step."

"You've got that right," Jenn readily agreed.

"And, he's a hunk."

Jennifer peeked under the canvas. "Mmmm . . . definitely yummy." She gave Lori a broad grin. "Actually, toots, I believe you're one hundred and ten percent right. What we have here is no less than the perfect man." With a wink, she said, "The kind of guy who listens and doesn't talk back."

TWO

The darkness was timeless, a place that was warm, where he floated between dreams and nothingness. Since the dreams were often painted in slashes of violence and rage, the escape he found in that dreamless nook was a welcome thing. It was there that Noble found peace.

At first he didn't overly appreciate the distant trickle of sound that came to him at odd intervals, intruding on his blissful, black slumber. But it grew increasingly familiar, moving in cadences not unlike speech. And yet he didn't hear words, but rather a resonance he could only interpret as shades of emotion.

"Damn, come on, will you? Just wake up instead of lying there like Sleeping Beauty waiting for a magic kiss. I'm lonely, you know? So damn lonely. And I'm sick and tired of sleeping alone—or make that not sleeping. See, I've got this problem with insomnia, ever since Mick died—but I already told you that, didn't I?"

By degrees, closer and closer the presence came. He sensed no menace in it, none whatsoever. On some instinctive level he felt himself responding to this presence, one that began to assume a distinctly feminine quality.

"So, tell me, how do I look? I'm all dressed up with no place to go, no thanks to you. I needed a night out, but nooo, I had a guilt trip that stopped me in my dancing boots. I certainly hope you appreciate me canceling out just in case you decide to start breathing again. And don't forget I'm spending all my lunch hours racing home to check on you. Ryan's giving me a hard time about that, you know. As for my other pals, they've got better things to do. Like dancing.

"Jeez, it's sweltering in here, no wonder my makeup's sliding off like butter on a griddle. Too warm for me, but maybe not warm enough for you. Better turn up the thermostat a notch and add a few bucks to my water bill. By the way, I hate to take showers and I really want my tub back. Nearly a week you've been sacked out in here and just look at this stuff all over the floor.

"Let's see . . . thermal blankets, check, a homemade crash cart that might earn me a Girl Scout badge in a pinch, double check. Time to check your vital signs again. Hmmm . . . blood pressure . . . forty over twenty. Probe in the ear, since I can't stick a thermometer under your tongue or up your butt . . . hey, great, seventy-two-point-five degrees . . . yep, you're warming up. And now roll the drums for a pulse . . . still not there. One more day, bronco, I'll give you one more day—okay, two days—and if I can't pick up some kind of a pulse, sorry, you're out of here.

"In the meantime, did I tell you about when I was a little girl and . . ."

A woman? Yes, he believed a woman must be keeping him company. If only he could wake up and enjoy the favors she might bestow once this endless night was over. Noble struggled for consciousness only to be weighted down by a force he was beginning to loathe.

Perhaps if he shifted, rolled atop her, her lullaby whispers would turn to sharp sighs of pleasure. Surely that would wake him up. With a strength of will that had served him well in life, he commanded his body to obey what his mind decreed. But his body felt sluggish and his will felt strangely weak, as if he hadn't used it in some time and it had gone to sleep along with the rest of him.

He embraced the destructive force that had thus far kept him alive, and it fed his determination to throw off the dark curtain of sleep. *Wake up, dammit. Wake up and fetch some blankets. Lord, but it's getting cold. Freezing cold.*

"Was that a pulse?" Lori wondered. "No, it couldn't be." She pressed his jugular harder. "Slow, faint, but yes . . . yes! I'm getting a pulse! Blood pressure? Sixty over forty . . . one more time to be sure. It's rising, rising fast, blood pressure eighty over fifty. And temperature, what is his temperature?

"Damn, quit shaking, would you?" she commanded herself when she nearly dropped the ear probe into the water. "Water, I need more hot water. But first I have to get his temperature. Why did I try to do this by myself? I need help. I need Ryan." Did she have time to dial 911?

"Temperature . . . eighty-four degrees—no, eighty-six. My God, I don't believe it, he just jerked." Lori felt her own pulse leap as she whispered in disbelief, "He's actually starting to move."

Was he ill? Noble wondered. Bloody hell, but he was freezing, the shudders inside him pounding to get out. And his feet, they felt as if a thousand pins were pricking them, making them twitch and tingle painfully.

"But he's not breathing. Oh shit, where's the hypo, the adrenaline?" Latching on to both, Lori groaned, suddenly unsure if she should give it to him. Would it be too much of a shock to his system? A doctor, he needed a doctor, not a nurse. Lord, she must have been out of her mind to think she could pull this off by herself. What if she resuscitated him only to kill him because she did something wrong? Could she be charged with murdering someone who'd been dead for a hundred years?

He couldn't catch his breath. Why couldn't he catch his breath? Was he dead? Was this hell? No, surely not. Not unless hell greeted its newcomers with a kiss.

A mouth was on his, a warm, soft, utterly feminine mouth. Her lips were open and she was breathing hard, sharing the flavor of cinnamon. Despite the needles of pain shooting through him, compounded by the heat of her breath, which filled his protesting lungs, Noble warmed to the kiss that surely had to be coming from a harlot. No proper woman would kiss a man with such

force and desperation. As for her pinching of his nose
. . . it must be a tart's trick unknown to him.

Suddenly she was no longer kissing him. She was
tearing at his shirt then pushing on his chest and
screaming, "Come on, damn you! Damn, don't you
leave me now!"

He wanted to say, he wouldn't dream of it. But the
words were trapped in his throat. While he struggled to
make them emerge she resumed pinching his nose and
kissed him even more fiercely.

Such a lusty wench! The chill was still making him
shiver, great shivers that erupted from the chest she was
now massaging. But he also felt a rising heat, fast seep-
ing around and through him.

Sensation spread as she stroked him almost everywhere—except for where he most wanted her to stroke.
He reached for her from what seemed to be an impossible distance.

"He's breathing now, really breathing," Lori
panted. In amazement, she realized he was trying to
move his hand toward her—but with little success. Her
heart sank. Nerve damage, how much had been done?
Had he lost the use of his fine-motor skills? Or, horror
of horrors, what if she'd revived him only to give him a
fate worse than death? Able to breathe, even think, but
unable to speak or move?

He seemed to be trying to release the gun she hadn't
been able to free from his paralytic grip. But he was
trying. Good, good. Only, he couldn't do it by himself.
Not good.

How very sweet she was, gripping his stiff hand and

relieving him of the familiar weight he wasn't inclined to give up. It was, after all, his gun. His gun? What in the blazes was he doing with a gun while keeping intimate company with a woman? Even if she was a harlot, it was imperative to apologize for such an unpardonable breach of etiquette.

His lips thoroughly warmed by her kissing, which he was eager to resume, and his halting breath coming fast, Noble forced a whisper past the rawness of his throat.

"My . . . lady. My . . . apologies."

"My God! Oh my God, you can talk!"

But of course he could talk, he wanted to tell her. And would have had those few words not taken such an uncommon amount of effort to get out. It was just as difficult to raise his eyelids so he might see her face. But she assisted him with that as well, gently lifting first one and then the other—and shining a sharp, irksome light into each.

She muttered softly to herself, sounding somewhat distressed. All in all, this was a most confusing encounter. Again, he tried to open his eyes, and managed a slitted gaze.

Noble beheld what appeared to be an angel. The light now shimmered behind her, like a halo around her golden hair. He thought it fashioned strangely, fringes wisping over her forehead, the rest cut short, reaching no farther than her shoulders. But it was lovely hair just the same, and he rather liked the peculiar way she had cut it.

He liked it almost as much as her eyes. They were blue and reminded him of periwinkles in bloom. She really had no need for the paint she wore, although ladies of the night often did rouge their cheeks, their lips, and even their nipples. But other than the smudges of color about her eyes, she wore no paint that he could readily see.

Her complexion was luminous but far from pale. There was a subtle fragility about her, but all in all, she was lacking in a delicate appearance. Even so, she was a handsome woman and the strength of her features appealed to him. Her mouth was especially exquisite. And how well she plied the skills of her trade, no teasing coquette in her kisses.

A violent shudder overtook him and his eyes slid shut as he battled with this strange malady that had a dreadful sense of timing. He heard her mumble something that sounded like "hypothermia" before she said with an unmistakable urgency, "I've got to get you out of these clothes, they're cooling off the water."

It was then that he realized he was in a long, deep tub. Fully clothed. Had he imbibed a bottle of whiskey before seeking the favors of this fetching woman? Though he wasn't inclined to drunkenness, it would explain much. Except for the racking shivers. They offered him little help as she cursed profusely and struggled to remove his coat.

He heard it thud onto the floor before she tugged at his shirt, which gaped open from her earlier romp upon his chest. He resisted her struggles, and she gave it up and went on. Off went his chaps, followed by his boots. No resistance from him with those; he raised his hips as best he was able and her fleet hands inched down his pants.

Despite great anticipation once she'd gotten them off, he was sorely vexed since the small effort had taxed him and his lax manhood was surely less than impressive.

Not that it dissuaded her, determined angel of the night that she apparently was. Noble surrendered to the luxury of her ministrations while he rested. The sound of running water, the hot feel of it, surprised him somewhat. Such modern conveniences were rare in these parts; clearly, this brothel was of a far higher quality than the one he usually visited.

Most definitely it was, he decided, when she sought to arouse him with an exotic array of sexual paraphernalia.

Nothing seeming quite real, despite the very real sensations she provoked as her fingertips stroked his ear and she pressed a blunt aparatus slightly inside, which faintly tickled. Removing it, she whispered, "Temperature rising, that's good, so good." And then she strapped a black cuff onto his upper arm, squeezed it tight with a peculiar attachment. Noble assumed it was some sort of bondage game she was playing, though for the life of him he couldn't say what the accessory, which ran from her ears to the silver piece she pressed to the inside of his arm, was for.

But it was over so quickly, he wondered if he'd imagined it all, if he was suffering from some sort of delirium. If so, he hoped never to recover—at least not until she finished with what was proving to be an incredibly stimulating massage.

Her hands were marvelous, rubbing his chest, his arms, even his feet, with a skillful fervor. Indeed, though the overly warm water was a balm to his chilled flesh, her touch was hot as a branding iron.

The chills began to subside. His shuddering breaths came easier. And though he still felt unaccountably weak, Noble could feel his strength growing.

He flexed a foot. Then crooked a knee. His arms felt equally stiff, but he moved them anyway, opening them to the sweet lady of tender ministrations.

She wrapped her arms around his neck, then pressed her fingertips to his throat. "Strong and steady. Sweetheart, you're gonna make it." She said the last with a heated passion as she pressed her lips to the pulse he could feel beating hard and quick, such was the magic of her kiss.

His loins responded, too, but not as well as he'd have liked. So it was with his mind, taking all of this in while a fuzziness dulled the edges. One thing was clear, however, this was no ordinary harlot.

"You're extraordinarily good at what you do," he told her with all sincerity. Though his voice was raspy, he was grateful for the ability to speak freely again. But most of all, he was grateful for this beguiling woman, the likes of which he'd never met. Not in England, and surely not in this primitive land of Alaska.

"Just doing my job," she said, her smile shining and bright. "But with you, it's more than that. We don't really know each other yet, but you're special to me."

"A mutual feeling, I promise you." Suddenly Noble wasn't at all sure that he wanted to share her. Women were at a premium and this one seemed an impressive cut above the rest—despite her rough language.

Had he ample gold in his discarded belongings to purchase her favors solely for himself? If not, he had hidden gold aplenty, and if he could woo her into agreeing . . . surely she would prefer the amorous attentions of one man to many.

"However I came to be here," he murmured, "I thank the gods for it." The glow of her smile warmed him and he had to wonder just how he *had* come to the good fortune of her presence. "Where am I?" he asked, hoping to nudge his memory.

She hesitated before saying, "Juneau."

Juneau! That would explain his lack of familiarity with the brothel he was in. A large ransom hung over his head here; it was not a place to linger. Noble suddenly stiffened.

She urged him deeper into the water and asked with concern, "Are you having trouble breathing? Is your heart starting to hurt?"

"If I'm having trouble catching my breath, it's because you take it away. And no, my heart feels no pain, but without doubt you could break it. Now please, cease speaking, I'm having enough difficulty thinking as it is."

He concentrated hard, and a flash of white came to him. And before that . . . before that, Bitter making a terrible sound then falling over a ledge. It had been night. Why had he not taken more precautions about the safety of their trail? Had they been trying to escape . . . pursuit?

Yes, yes, it was coming back to him now. The posse and their gunfire too close at his back. What was to be his last bank robbery, gone awry.

"How was I found?" he demanded shortly.

"You were . . . you were buried deep and at first thought dead. But someone believed you might live against the odds, and so you were brought here."

He didn't have to think hard to know who that someone was. He'd warned Attu not to follow him, but when had his stalwart friend ever listened? Attu, his dearest and most trusted friend, who had an insatiable taste for harlots.

But he wouldn't share this one even with Attu.

"I presume that we have a mutual friend in Attu. Where is he now?"

"He's—he's . . . I'm sorry, but he's gone."

"Ah, back to Skagway to make excuses for my absence." The agility of his mind returning, Noble pieced the logical sequence of events together: Attu had trailed him, dug him out of the snow—no doubt nearly freezing himself in the process—then returned to the closest town due to his weakened condition. The local doctor would bear no trust; a whorehouse was far more reliable.

"Tell me," Noble asked urgently, "how long have I been here?"

Again she hesitated. "Nearly a week."

A week! No wonder his dreaming and dark lapses had seemed to go on forever.

"I must go." Noble made to rise, only to find the woman pressing him back. He cursed softly. But he didn't bother to apologize, given her own propensity for swearing.

"You can't go now," she protested.

"Allow me a fortnight to see to my responsibilities and I'll come fetch you." As for the bank, he would wait out the winter to rob it. Yet he could not wait that long to claim this sweet, lusty lady. "Have you a horse that you could lend me? I promise not to steal it." Despite the frantic need to find his friend, Noble permitted himself a strained chuckle at the small joke he'd made. She did not laugh with him.

Rather, she said fervently, "I want you to stay with me. You *have* to—at least for a little while. If you go now, you won't be safe, and I'd never forgive myself if something bad happened to you. Please, don't try to leave."

Her palms gripped his shoulders and she pressed him deeper into the tub. Water sloshed over the side and he noticed her white blouse was molded to a pair of breasts so enticing that he was sorely tempted to linger.

A short time would not make much difference. But he could afford only a few stolen moments.

"My good woman," Noble murmured, "I find your character as exceptional as your feminine charms. Unwise though it is, I'll dally with you for as long as I dare." Already he dreaded their parting. But he would make such exquisite love to her first, she wouldn't hesitate to promise to save her favors for him, and only him, until he returned to claim her.

Her lips seemed to beg for a kiss and Noble traced the full sweep of her bottom lip. It quivered softly beneath the pad of his thumb as she whispered, "For the moment why don't we dally together over a bowl of chicken soup?"

THREE

"Your offer of soup is most kind," he replied in a low, roughened voice Lori likened to raw silk. "However, I find that my appetite requires more tempting fare."

Lori was at once enchanted by his quaint, eloquent way of speaking and slightly unnerved by the smoldering glint in his eyes. They were an unusual, riveting shade of gray, reminding her of gunmetal. His unwavering gaze seemed to pin her in place beside the claw-footed tub at the same time it lured her to lean closer and press her palm to his chest.

His heart beat in a steady rhythm, assuring her that he was unbelievably, miraculously alive. She assured herself further that the crisis was truly over by giving in to the temptation of tentatively exploring his chest. Beneath the dense mat of dark hair, his skin was warm, his muscles taut and firm. Without her conscious consent her fingertips wandered, lightly touched the tip of a dark brown nipple.

One side of his mouth crooked up in a devilishly sexy half smile. Definitely alive. Lori's heart caught and so did her breath. The sound of her pulse swelled in her ears. It mingled with the thickening silence, carried on sultry tendrils of steam.

She tried for a hospitable tone, but her voice emerged throaty and carried an undercurrent of innuendo. "If you're not in the mood for soup, what sounds good to you?"

"Your voice sounds lovely. And strangely familiar." Lines of concentration creased his prominent brow, which glistened, droplets trickling from his dark brown hair. "I'm sure that I'd remember had we met before. And yet, it seems like I know you. Such a mystery, is it not?"

As with his previous questions, she was carefully ambiguous in her reply. "Not such a mystery, really. I talked to you a lot while you were . . . unconscious." Her deepest, darkest confessions coming back to her, she laughed, embarrassed, and ducked her head.

Only to take in the flat plane of his abdomen. Unable to stop herself, she glanced lower and saw that he was partially aroused. Not fully resuscitated yet, but showing impressive signs of life. She jerked up her gaze.

And encountered his amused, intimate regard.

Lori was suddenly uncomfortable—with their compromising positions; with the atmosphere, charged with expectation. But most of all with her awareness of him as a man whose nearness was awakening something inside her, a miracle in itself. The persona he projected was so strong and compelling she could hardly think past the clamoring impulses she had thought buried with Mick. Now they were coming back to life with a desperate vengeance, resurrected by the man she had labored, prayed, to save.

It had been so long, how good it was to feel the tug of desire again. At the moment she didn't even care if it sprang from the ordeal they'd shared, the bond she'd forged with him during the nights she'd watched over him, pouring out her heart for hours on end.

"When you talked to me," he said into the lengthening silence, "did you tell me secrets?"

"Let's just say that you were such a good listener, I did a lot of gut spilling." Lori could feel her cheeks flush. "Pretty messy. Hopefully you won't remember anything I said."

"Hopefully, I will." His smile deepened. "But have no fear, your secrets are safe with me. Just as you've proved that mine are with you. A rare and promising beginning to our relationship, don't you agree?"

Their relationship, she knew, was infinitely more complex and far reaching than he could possibly grasp. How in the world she could prepare him for the reality of his situation, she had no idea. As for how he would take it, his reaction could range from shock to disbelief to rage—maybe all three.

The longer she could avoid the inevitable, the better off he'd be. After the physical trauma he'd suffered, the last thing he needed was for her to heap on distress or confusion by asking him about the secrets he himself had spoken of. Whatever they were, they couldn't be half as horrible as discovering that all his friends and family were long gone.

Lori hurt for him already. He would need a friend, a good one, to get through what lay ahead. And she was it.

"My name's Lori," she said, extending her hand.

He brushed a kiss to her knuckles. "I'm charmed."

Deciding that she'd better get this lady-killer out of the tub and into some clothes before she said or did something she'd be sorry for later, she tried to pull back her hand. He tightened his hold and stroked a finger over her wrist.

"Forget the soup. I'll go see what's in the—" *Fridge.* Catching herself, she quickly amended, "Pantry. While I do that you can dry off. Think you can manage by yourself?"

"Perhaps." He returned her hand to his chest and lifted an eyebrow, suggestively. "Perhaps not."

The thought of running a towel over those tough, lean muscles of his stirred her, made her ache in hidden places of both heart and heat. She was experiencing a sweet revival, and though good sense warned her not to, Lori offered hopefully, "I'll be glad to help."

"How accommodating you are, my dear." He wrapped the endearment around his tongue in an easy, intimate way that rendered her spellbound as he led her palm to his shoulder and slid his own to her waist. "I'll accept your offer of help. But first, a request."

Anything, she wanted to say. Lori was drowning in his slitted gaze and getting dangerously close to making a request of her own—*kiss me*—when he cinched his hold.

"And just what might your request be?" she whispered.

"I wish for you to come join me." He hauled her over, and she fell in with a splash and a gasp.

He cupped her behind and pushed up so that her breasts bobbed against his chest. Water streaming down her face, she sputtered, "What—what do you think you're doing?"

"Thinking is the business of philosophers. Doing is the business between us." He hiked up her full denim skirt while his mouth seemed to be in more places at once than was humanly possible.

Biting her chin, sipping at her neck, tonguing her earlobe, he whispered hotly, "As you can see, my strength is fast returning. And none too soon. You are without doubt, the most delectable morsel of femininity to grace my company and straddle my hips in what seems forever. But alas, our time is short. Please, allow me to show my gratitude for your many kindnesses before I take my leave."

Lori wasn't sure whether to slap his face or beg him to be more than generous in his show of mind-reeling, pulse-pounding thanks. She commanded herself to think, to get this crazy situation under control while she still could.

"If—if you really want to show your gratitude . . ." *More, please more.* Her starved senses clamored for attention. So did her professional concerns. How could she be sure that he was entirely stable? What if his heart, his respiration, couldn't handle the excitement her own body was hard-pressed to handle itself?

"You need only tell me what it is you wish for, and I'll grant your slightest whim," he assured her in a rich, gravelly voice. "But while you consider your desires, you won't mind if I indulge one of my own, will you?"

Did he mean to ravish her? Her heart thumping like mad, Lori was terribly afraid that he would—only when he fingered her wet bangs, she was jolted by a distinct disappointment that ravishment was apparently not to be her fate.

"I'm quite taken with your hair," he explained. "Fascinated, really. How you've cut it—I've never seen anything quite so striking. And the color is lovely. Yes, very lovely . . . as are you."

For a moment she could only stare at him, her mind whirling on tiptoes of delight, her body tingling from the unexpected tenderness of his touch.

"I'm glad you like it," she said softly. *Soft.* He made her feel soft inside and feminine all over.

"Oh, but I do. Almost as much as I like the feel of you under my hands, the sound of those catching little breaths I hear. In truth, I like everything about you. Never has a woman so completely engaged my attention. Alas, I could very easily be smitten with you."

"You're dangerous," she whispered, certain of that even if she was no longer certain of anything else.

"Indeed," he agreed, playing with the ends of her hair. "But you needn't fear me, though there are others who should."

A sudden darkness lurked in his hooded gaze. What

she glimpsed was brutal, merciless, cold. Lori shivered. It was a lethal, stalking kind of danger that went far beyond the sensual danger he posed to a woman as vulnerable as she. *Who was he?* Part of her was desperate to find out; part of her prayed she would never know.

"You're so still, so quiet," he said, his gaze mellowing on her. "What are you thinking?"

"It's strange, but I get the feeling . . . well, almost like you're two different people in one."

"But of course I am." He frowned. "I assumed that Attu told you."

"Your—your friend didn't really tell me anything. I only knew you were in need of help and you're lucky—"

"Lucky Luke," he interjected, chuckling. "Such a lackluster name, don't you think?"

"It's okay." Images of cards and drawn guns came at her.

"So, Attu failed to mention my real name?" At her nod, he bowed toward her—which put his lips a whisper from hers and caused his hips to rise slightly. She stifled a gasp, and then a moan, when he nuzzled into the juncture of her thighs. What had been only half-alive was fully alive now.

He murmured a sigh of satisfaction, then said with a gallant air, "Allow me to introduce myself. Noble Zhivago, barrister."

Zhivago, that was Russian, wasn't it? And yet his accent pegged him as a proper Brit. While she found herself puzzling his nationality Lori was struck by the absurd politeness of their exchange in an anything but polite position.

"You're a lawyer?" she asked, unable to subdue a grin.

"It seems you find my occupation amusing," he noted with such seriousness that she couldn't hold back her laughter. "I fail to understand the cause for your humor, but whatever it is, I'm glad of it. You have a truly delightful laugh. I can only hope you indulge the sound often . . . Lori."

His words touched her, deeply, and she quickly sobered. But a warm, happy feeling remained as she confessed, "Actually, I don't laugh, really laugh, very often. At least I haven't in recent years. Noble." She liked the way his name tasted, how the resonance of it lingered on her tongue. "Noble," she said again. "A wonderful name. It suits you."

"Thank you. I'm sure my parents would be pleased to think they had chosen well." That frightening something she'd glimpsed earlier flashed without warning in his eyes. Then, like quicksilver, it was gone, replaced by a silvery gleam as he urged her deeper into the saddle of his thighs.

"Now tell me what you found to be of such amusement," he murmured. "Perhaps I shall laugh with you, then. I fear that my laughter, like yours, comes far too rarely."

"I—uh, I don't think it would be so funny now." Lori swallowed, her throat gone dry. "In fact, I think it would be a good idea if we got out of the tub. The water's starting to cool off."

"The water does grow tepid. My desire for you, however, is quite another matter." His soft bite of her bottom lip coincided with his smooth glide of her hand between them. Down and down he led her, unresisting, touching the taut muscles of his chest, the sweeping width of hair that slid ever downward, thinning, then thickening in an altogether too male area of his body.

There, he paused and let go of her hand. He cupped her where no man had touched her since Mick had died. This, *this* was life, what she felt unfurling inside her. And how hungry she was for it, to feel the rapture again, to know she was a woman with needs and wants and dreams.

She seemed to be in a dream, touching and being touched by a dark stranger who whispered, "How long has it been since a man cared more about your pleasure than his?"

"A very long time. So long that I'd forgotten how beautiful something like this could be." She stared at him, her heart in her eyes, and felt the threat of tears behind them. "I don't know you, not really, but I do know you must be a very rare man. You have to be to make me feel the way I do now. Special and pretty, inside and out."

"But of course you are," he assured her with such sincerity that she had no doubt he meant it. "Whatever fate brought you to ever question it is no less than a travesty. I, too, have been the victim of circumstances beyond my control. And so we do what demands to be done."

He kissed her softly, much too briefly, but it was a potent kiss just the same. The hint of tobacco was on his breath; it fanned her parted lips, which yearned for a deeper mating. "I make no demands on you," he said quietly. "My only wish is that you might need something of me. Do you?"

"I . . ." She did need something from him. The passion, the fire, the sheer joy of being held and touched by a man who made her feel again. She needed reality to slip away, to be foolish and give in to this reckless abandon. "I do," she answered.

"Then by all means, tell me."

Unable to speak aloud what she couldn't admit to herself any more than she could deny it, she delved lower, wrapped her shaking palm around his length. A faraway voice called to her, warning her with a single word, *insane*.

But what a fine madness it was. Waves of sensation rippled from her hand and spread like a match put to dry grass after years of a drought.

"Dear God," she breathed out in a broken whisper. Her belly clutched; her womb reached for what she held.

She began to shake, shake all over, and Lori was suddenly frightened by the quaking of her body. It was making demands, urgent, uncompromising demands that trampled her search for a fragment of lost reason. *What was happening to her?*

She didn't know, but something was taking her over and she was desperate to regain some sense of control.

She heard a distant sound and she thought he must be groaning. And perhaps he was, but the pitch she heard was too high, a whimper that went on and on and became an endless moan. And then she knew it was her, moaning and choking on sobs while her thighs jerked open. And she was frantically rubbing against his palm, trying to push him in and starting to cry because something was in the way, something besides his petting hand.

Her panty hose, she thought it was her panty hose. She couldn't release him long enough to do it herself and so she pleaded, "Take them off. Tear them, rip them, I don't care. Just please, get the damn things off!"

Her head fell back and she rocked faster, harder, while his own hips were too still and his hands stroked her too softly. One in her hair and the other palming her through the hose, he made no effort to remove.

Why was he taunting her this way? Why was he murmuring quiet, comforting words while she wanted to scream her frustration at him?

And then her body was screaming for release, for an end to the pain. She was racked with it, her hollow womb pleading to be touched and filled. And then something broke, shattered within. It was tearing her apart, turning her inside out, then leaving her to crumple with nothing to hold on to. Nothing to feel except the release of an inner fist quivering in exquisite sensation.

But the rest of her felt bruised, battered from the assault of a ferocious inner storm that had taken her over, used her, then flung her carelessly aside.

She was left in pieces, her pride thrown away.

Lori was desperate to find it. She was desperate to crawl into a dark corner and hide. Far, far away from here, where she lay sprawled in a messy, sobbing heap on top of a near stranger who was soothing her with a tender, consuming embrace. His hand stroked her hair. He pressed his lips to her temple and made a "shhhh, shhhh" sound of comfort.

All of her clothes were on, even her boots, and yet never had Lori felt so naked, so rawly exposed.

"My lady," he whispered. She turned her face as far away as she could, only for him to grip her jaw insistently and turn her to face him. "Look at me," he firmly demanded.

"No. I—I'm sorry, but I just can't."

"But, why? Are you angry with me because I didn't—"

"Please, don't remind me. I feel humilated enough as it is. But no, I'm not angry with you. Just with myself."

Even breathing seemed to take all the energy she had, but she felt for the tub's edge and tried to crawl out.

His hard clamp on her wrist coincided with the grip of his thighs, the tug of his hand in her hair. Forcing her eyes open, she winced at the concern in his gaze. "Please, Noble, let me go. I need to be alone."

He shook his head slowly, irrevocably. "You are not a harlot, are you?"

FOUR

A harlot? Struggling to remain calm, she said, "No, I am not a harlot. Even if I acted like one."

He laughed softly at that. "My dear, please rest assured that in no way did you conduct yourself as a harlot—even one with rudimentary experience. I hope you will forgive me."

"Forgive you?" she repeated, dumbfounded. "For what?"

"For mistaking your occupation as one you couldn't possibly fulfill," he said. "After all, you can't touch and not feel, can you?" When she didn't answer, he continued. "Please know, had I sooner realized you were a woman of virtue, I never would have attempted to compromise you."

Lori was no less than amazed that he considered her a woman of virtue—which she was—after she'd all but forced herself on him. Unable to bear the lengthening silence further, she asked unevenly, "Anything else?"

"I regret my refusal to compromise your virtue." He brushed his fingers against the nylon from her thighs to her hips. "When you demanded me to remove your pantalets, honor demanded that I not. And now my body demands to know what stupidity possessed me to refuse you, much to the detriment of us both."

Lori's cheeks flared hot, scalding hot, and more than anything she wanted to go under the water and never come up. But instead she forced herself to meet his probing gaze and remain still as he fingered the elastic at her waist.

Noble's brow gathered into a network of fine lines.

"Never have I encountered such a clever work of underclothing before. Are they some new invention imported from France, perhaps?"

Had panty hose originated in France? Lori had no idea, but for now, she decided, panty hose had most definitely come from France, not from the clearance rack at her local department store.

At her nod, he said, "You intrigue me. Everything about you seems so honest, and yet you're a mire of contradictions. For a truth, I cannot understand why such a clearly decent woman would allow me the liberties reserved for a husband. And *why* would you paint your face?"

Paint her face? Lori decided he meant what little was left of the makeup she'd applied hours ago, thinking she'd meet the gang at the Kick and Kaboodle. But thank heavens she hadn't been able to bring herself to leave Noble; and thank heavens she'd dressed in her country-and-western dancing clothes. Between her long denim skirt, simple white blouse, and boots, she could pass for a woman from Noble's time—except for her makeup.

"I paint my face because I think it makes me look better. And you didn't take any more liberties than I did. I'm a widow, Noble. And I guess you could say I was very much in need of a reminder that I'm still alive even if my husband isn't."

"I see." The look he gave her was accepting, but dissatisfied, as if he were playing second lead and was accustomed to commanding the stage.

"Next question," she prompted.

"Not a question, an observation. You're wealthy."

"I am?" When he frowned, she quickly amended, "Well, yes, I am. How did you know?"

"How could I not know? You have a fine porcelain tub, running water, the most modern of fixtures." He gestured to her antiquated bathroom. It complemented the furnishings throughout her house—secondhand vintage, reupholstered in jeweled tones. The hardwood floors with scattered tapestry rugs lent warmth—and contributed to the appearance of a bygone era.

"I live comfortably," she hedged, wondering how long the surroundings would fool Noble. Not nearly long enough, that was for sure. One look at her kitchen and he'd freak. For that matter, all he had to do was get a gander at her TV and be plunged into his own personal episode of *The Twilight Zone*.

Exhausting and mind-blowing as the night had already been, it was sure to be a walk in the park compared with the dreaded inevitable. She wasn't ready to handle this any more than Noble could be. But she had to say something, do something, to ease him into it before she dropped the bomb.

An idea came to her. "If you'll give me a minute to change, I'll bring you some dry clothes." Contemporary fashion, a good place to start.

"It's rather dubious that I can fit into any of yours." His gaze dropped to her soaked blouse and lingered.

Lori could feel her nipples tauten. She had forgotten her shame, her distress for having come so completely undone. Confronted with both, she wanted none of either. Noble was a special man and he created some very special reactions in her. What he had given her, what she had greedily taken, was a part of her life back. There was no shame in that.

"I have a few things that belonged to my husband. He was a good man, a very generous man. If he were here, he'd be the first to insist on sharing what he had with you."

"Even his wife?" At her striken expression, Noble quickly said, "That was unpardonable. Forgive me."

"But you said it. I want to know why."

"A fair demand," he conceded. "Though I have no right, I'm rather jealous. And it grieves me to think you might still regret the pleasure you found with me. I suppose I was simply asking aloud what I believed you were asking yourself in silence."

"You must have excellent hearing," she admitted. "I did, and still do, love my husband. But Mick is dead and he's not coming back. What happened tonight happened—and I'm not sorry for it." She summoned up a tentative smile. "Now that we've got that settled, let's get out of this tub and pick up our conversation over a bowl of homemade chicken soup." Uh-oh. Where would they eat it?

The dining room was safe. But she had to keep him out of the kitchen. And the living room. And her bedroom—and not just because she had an electric clock and a phone in there.

"Homemade soup? But what other kind would you have?"

"Uh . . . There's good homemade and there's bad homemade. Mine's good. And only the best for you."

"So it would seem, given the luxury of your company." He allowed her to gain her footing on the floor, then took the hand she extended.

Though she tried not to look, she found herself staring at the considerable evidence of his unsated arousal as he hoisted himself up. Standing, he seemed even more powerful. Almost a head taller, his great, brawny chest filled her vision. She wanted to pull off his open, soaked shirt for a better view but knew that would be courting trouble. Let it drip on the already wet floor, she decided.

Refusing herself the temptation to stroke his chest— or the greater temptation that resided lower—Lori quickly handed him a nearby towel.

"What in the bloody blazes is this?" he asked, staring at the big pink flamingo printed in the center of the terry cloth.

Tell him, dammit, just tell him the year 2000 is just

around the bend and neon's in. "It's—it came from France with my pantalets."

Brrinng. Brrrinng.

"That sound, what is it?"

"It's, uh . . ." The phone quit ringing. Cursing herself for a coward, Lori said in a rush, "My clock chiming. It came from France, too."

Noble's brow furrowed. "It would seem that you have an uncommon number of imported possessions. Was your husband a smuggler, perchance?"

"No, he was—" *A policeman.* What did they call policemen in Noble's day? Since she had no idea, Lori ad-libbed. "Like you, he was involved with the law." Good, she thought. Lawyers and policemen had plenty of contact with each other.

"Ah, now I begin to understand why you so generously took me in. However, I'm greatly puzzled why Attu failed to mention your acquaintance to me. Were you just recently introduced?" At her quick nod, he said, "That is my good fortune," and turned his attention to the task of drying off, briskly, as if he were in a hurry.

Lori told herself to go change, but she remained rooted in place, watching him sweep the cloth over his magnificent chest. Noble looked up. An intimate smile framed his lips as he caught her artlessly gawking.

"How thoughtless of me. Seeing to myself while you shiver." Ever so softly he caressed the towel over her cheeks, her neck, and then the wet fabric clinging to her arms. "My lady . . . Lori. Leaving you will be enormously difficult for me. Nevertheless, I've stayed too long. I'll accept your offer of clothing and a bowl of soup. Should you have jerky or dried fruit you can spare me, I'll be most grateful. Even more so for the loan of a horse."

"Anything that I've got, you can have. But—"

"It is you whom I want. I must see you again, and when I do—soon, very soon—it will be with the most honorable of intentions. For now, however, I have no choice but to leave. Attu's life might very well hang in the balance."

Steeling herself, Lori said somberly, "I hate to tell you this, Noble, believe me I do. But you have no reason to leave. Your friend Attu, he's dead." *And all the other friends and family you once had.* How could she possibly tell him something so devastating, heap heartache on top of the heartache she witnessed now?

A sharp, tortured sound caught in Noble's throat. His eyes grew misty, the color of an overcast sky. Then swiftly his gaze hardened and his eyes turned a chilling shade of cold steel. His soft touch to her arm became a hard clench. Gone was the gentleman of refinement. This man was scary.

"I'm really sorry about your friend, Noble," Lori said, her voice trembling.

"Not half as sorry as the bastards who took him down will be. Once I'm done with them, they'll consider hell a merciful reprieve."

From the brutal rage marring his face, Lori knew that whoever those bastards were, they were lucky to be dead already. She wondered how a man of such breeding, a lawyer, had come to make dangerous enemies—

who couldn't be half as dangerous as Noble clearly was himself.

Would he direct some of that terrible anger toward her in response to the shattering news she had to give? Quite possibly he would. But if she could connect with him on a deeper level first, forge a sense of kinship, surely he would be less upset. With that hope, she opened herself to him, let him touch a very private part of herself, a part that understood the destructive emotions she saw in him now.

Her gaze full of empathy, Lori cupped his cheek.

"I know what you're feeling, Noble, and it's a terrible thing. But hate has a way of eating a person alive, consuming them and taking over, until it poisons even the good things left in life. In the end, the person you're really hurting is yourself. Let it go."

He turned his lips into her palm. A soft, lingering kiss, and then he moved away. With the towel cinched at his waist and covering his thighs, he paced the small area of floor, reminding her of a sleek, lethal animal trapped in a cage.

"Your words bear consideration, and without doubt they hold much truth. I cannot, however, relinquish my thirst for justice, nor my sense of honor. If a man will not uphold the dignity of his family name, then he is no man at all." He speared her with a fierce, prideful gaze. "I am a man, Lori."

And what a man he was. Never had she beheld a man such as this, a magnificent warrior who thirsted for blood even as he held to his principles. Lord, but he must have been hell to take on in a courtroom. *Lord, but he must be the devil in bed.* And Lord, she'd better stop thinking such things and get him into those clothes that were sure to raise his suspicions.

"Stay with me tonight, Noble. We'll have dinner while we talk . . . about all kinds of things. I'm really tired of eating alone and I'd love nothing better than to have you for company. Besides, you've had a hard time of it and I'm sure you could use the rest."

"My dear, keeping company with you provokes many ideas, but rest is not among them." His low chuckle was seductive. "However, I accept your kind offer. In return, I offer you the promise of my protection—which includes guarding you from my less honorable nature."

Lori was a little sorry to hear this, but she delighted in his chivalrous flair. It induced her to indulge a feminine skill she hadn't tried out in years.

"My, what a gentleman you are," she replied, almost tempted to curtsy. "You have quite a way with women, Mr. Zhivago. I'm not entirely sure that you're safe with me."

She half expected him to laugh. Or maybe one up her in their flirtatious exchange. What she didn't anticipate was his head-to-toe devouring regard. It gave her the shivers.

She shivered even more when he bent low and whispered in her ear, "A gentleman I might appear to be, but appearances are often deceiving. I would very much like to have my way with you, and my way would be anything but gentlemanly."

His low growl of warning caused her to step back.

She slipped on the wet floor and he caught her with an arm around her waist, a hand bracing the pedestal sink.

Noble went still. Too still.

She turned her head, followed the path of his shrewd gaze. It was on her electric toothbrush.

Oh no. Doomsday was here and she was nowhere near ready to take it on. And she certainly wasn't ready to take on a man who obviously thrived on reason and control—both of them about to be ripped from his grip.

FIVE

He narrowed his eyes at the anomaly he saw, and then at Lori. "What is this?" Noble demanded.

"It's—it's a . . . fancy toothbrush. From—"

"France?" he supplied as he urged her aside and lifted what bore only a minor resemblance to a toothbrush. There were bristles, but they were made of a white, unnatural substance he had never seen. And they were attached to a sleek, long, thick handle, possessing a most peculiar veneer. On it was a flat square with arrows beside it, pointing to the words *on* and *off*.

When he made to push the square to the on sign, Lori grabbed his hand.

"Don't," she said frantically.

He shook off her grip, and with an upward press of his thumb, the instrument began to hum, pulsating in his palm, which had begun to tremble slightly without assistance. The bristles quivered and so did his stomach.

He had grown beyond fear of man and death. But

this, this perversity of nature, left him chilled. He instinctively threw down what had to be an illusion. The object landed in the porcelain sink and gyrated against a round gold circle. It was then that he noticed the spigot had an attachment that he pulled up and down; as he did so the gold circle went up and down too. It acted as a cork, he realized, but he'd never seen a cork such as this.

"Noble? Noble, look—" He shook off her frantic grip on his wrist and went to the tub. He repeated the motions, amazed, stunned by what his eyes insisted was true but his reason insisted was not.

Sweeping his gaze to what he had first thought an exotic chair with a slop jar housed in the seat, he saw that it also had a suspicious lever.

"Why didn't I notice that before?" he asked himself aloud. Then to Lori, he said decisively, "I've allowed you to distract me too much as it is. Move away."

She tried to block him and he thrust her aside, intent on confronting the throne in this delusive setting. He took a lurching step and his bare foot bumped the pile of devices he had thought to be aids for arousal.

"Noble, please, you have to listen to me—"

"Listen to you? To what shall I be listening? An hallucination? Yes. Yes, that's what you are." Dear God, please let all of this be exactly that. Let him be trapped in a bizarre delirium that had him fabricating the array of objects slithering like vipers around his feet, suddenly bearing no resemblance to sexual bed toys.

That he had allowed her to put these foreign perversities on him . . . he shuddered.

Noble swiped at his arm where she had put the cuff, feeling as if he had been violated by an obscenity of nature. Searching for something, anything that might give him a sense of reality, he spied his gun. With a desperate urgency, he bent to retrieve it. Only to encounter Lori's boot stamping down on the familiar metal before he could claim it.

"My gun," he snarled at her. "Remove your foot from my gun."

"I'm sorry, Noble. But I can't let you have your gun. Please, sit down, catch your breath, and try to relax while I explain everything as best I can."

"Explain everything?" he challenged, his eyes wild and wary. "Yes, please do. Explain this." He kicked aside the tools of her nightmarish trade. Everything about him, even time, seemed to expand and contract while he struggled for a sense of balance. Whether it was seconds or hours, he didn't know, but at last he slammed his hand down on the lever attached to the ornate slop jar.

No slop jar had a hole in the bottom of it. No slop jar made a sucking noise and contained a swirling pool of water that disappeared then resurged as if by magic.

"And explain this." He raced back to the sink, but his feet seemed to be moving in slow motion, taking forever to get him to the elongated stained-glass fixture above the basin.

When he struck his fist against it, not only did the overlong light beneath shine too brightly to be a dull, flickering bulb, but the fixture itself lacked the properties of glass. The casing was too thin and had a texture unknown to him. It was attached to a wall, which was made of an equally strange substance. No paper covered the wood. In fact there was no wood to be seen at all.

He put his fist through a thin, glossy white . . . he had no idea what this enigma was doing passing for a wall. Noble quickly jerked away from it and put his palm to the light source that could be no more real than the burning sensation it elicited. No, he couldn't really be burned. No more than he could bleed—though blood appeared to spurt from the opposite palm he slammed against the trick fixture until it shattered.

"You're bleeding. Let me look at that and—"

"Get away from me," he snapped. Knocking her hand away, he quickly retrieved the gun left on the floor. Training it on her, he said in a lethal whisper, "Stay where you are, you demon of the dark, seducing me with your feminine wiles. I know where I must be. I am either trapped in a nightmare or I'm in hell. Whichever it is, leave me be."

Backing out of the room, Noble tried to ignore her pleas that were so distressed, so absolutely human, he felt more threatened than ever. He made his way quickly down the corridor and a flight of stairs. His surroundings should have been askew, wavering and insubstantial, not possessing the solidity of a hardwood floor that supported his racing feet.

And why wasn't her voice calling after him a haunting echo instead of a desperate cry of his name as he found himself in what appeared to be a parlor not so unlike his own.

With his eyes darting around the room, Noble saw

several strange items illuminated by a lamp. He didn't bother to investigate. Instead, he hurried toward the curtains. Jerking them back, he prepared to plummet headfirst through the enormous window, praying the jolt would awaken him and he'd be in his own parlor, not this house of horrors he was desperate to escape.

Just before he lunged, two bright lights appeared. They looked like monstrous eyes glowing in the dark, streaking in his direction. And attached to those eyes was a lumbering carcass he could liken only to a roaring dragon.

A nightmare within, a nightmare without. Noble threw himself to the side, away from the window, as if dodging a bullet.

How gladly he would take it. At least bullets were real.

His hip collided with a huge black box. Rounding the newest anomaly in this otherworldly place, Noble pointed his gun at it.

Cautiously, he scanned an assortment of buttons. He reached for the flat black button marked *on*.

"Noble, no!"

He ignored her imaginary voice and slapped aside her phantom grip trying to stay his hand.

Noble pressed the button. The big black box lit up and he saw the impossible. A woman with nothing on except for the briefest of attire covering her breasts, her maidenhood.

Her voice spilled out with anger and fear, as if she were speaking to him, not the menacing man who was also inside the box leering at her.

"Sail your ship wherever you like, you bastard. Just don't ever try to drop your anchor in this port again." And then the man shoved her to what appeared to be white sand. With an evil smile he said, "Such a shame you found out the reason I ever dropped it in the first place. Sorry, babe, but you know too much. You're dead."

Appalled by what he witnessed, Noble took aim at the bastard who began to strangle the helpless woman.

"No!" Lori shouted as Noble shot the despicable man.

Glass and sparks flew out where the people had been, popping and hissing noises replacing their voices.

And then, silence. Absolute silence. Except for the pounding beat of his heart, filling his ears and all but drowning out the wheeze of Lori's labored panting.

Even with the distance of several yards between them, he could see her shaking.

Her voice trembled even more as she said, very slowly, "Please, Noble. Put . . . down . . . the gun."

He threw it across the room and advanced on her with a menace equal to hers.

Clamping her shoulders, he glared at her with a rage he clung to. Rage was familiar; this fear he felt, fear of the unknown, was not familiar, and he loathed it.

"Who are you?" he demanded.

"Like I said, I—I'm Lori. Lori Morgan."

"Demon or angel?" When her mouth moved but no words emerged, he shook her. "This is hell, isn't it?"

"No! No, you're not in hell. You're in Juneau."

"Close enough." He ridiculed her sad attempt at

humor with a harsh bark of laughter. And then he shook her again while he dug his fingers into what felt to be flesh, soft and real and more dream than nightmare. Lowering his face until his nose nearly met hers, he said, "You will tell me the truth. Am I dead? Or am I only dreaming that I am?"

"You—you're not dead. But . . . you were. See, it's like this. You went to sleep and then you woke up. Say, about a hundred years later?"

Impossible. Giving himself up to the delirium or dream or death or whatever this perverse thing was, Noble played along with her.

"And just who should I have to thank for my journey into this netherworld of curious absurdities?"

Lori paused, then said, "Me."

Noble glowered at this angel of destruction, obviously sent to make him pay for the past sins he wasn't in the least bit sorry for.

"Tell you what, why don't I make a fire?" She smiled uncertainly then turned in the direction of a fireplace. Trusting her intent no more than he did his surroundings, Noble grabbed her back, pulled her against him.

He studied her wide-eyed, unblinking gaze. He lowered his own to the swell of her breasts, which heaved up and down against his chest in time to her strident panting. And then he brought his attention to her mouth. Open. Her lips veritably quivered.

She was frightened. Of him. Could it be that she was . . . human?

Demons could lie, but a human response could not.

Bent on finding out the truth of her humanity or lack of it, he bit carefully into her quivering bottom lip, poised to pull away should a forked tongue lick out at him.

When she whimpered softly rather than hissed, he tested the softness of her lips, inside and out.

For a certainty, they possessed a luscious, giving texture he was beginning to believe he had not imagined before, nor was he imagining now. Just to be sure, he crushed her lips with his, thrust his tongue inside her mouth, explored every nook and cranny within while her own tongue timidly swept over and around his.

It was a search for lies and truths he was after, not words. He was a master at twisting them to cast doubt on what was true and belief in what was not. The answers he gleaned from her response were too needfully raw to be anything but human and unquestionably honest.

From her hesitant then aggressive return of his kiss, to her palms that no longer pushed him away but clenched into his back, she left him with little doubt that this was indeed real. And even what small doubt remained vanished with the feel of her nails biting into his shirt and streaking a path so feverish he would likely bear her marks despite the protection of fabric.

Noble broke away. Horrified, amazed, by the realization that he was not delusional, he was not trapped in a nightmare, nor was he in hell. He was in a pocket of time outside his own, in a place beyond dreams or the wildest of waking imaginings.

"You're real," he whispered as Lori reluctantly released her hold. Glancing about the room, then shutting his eyes against it, he said what had to be true but what he couldn't believe. "All of this, it's real."

"Yes," she answered him unevenly. "It is real, Noble. All of it. You're not dreaming and you're not in hell. You're alive and so am I."

Still fighting disbelief, he stared at her. A woman. But not just any woman. A stunning and very much alive woman who was trying very hard not to cry while she traced her swollen lips with a shaking fingertip.

"I know it's a lot to absorb, but try to understand as much as you can. You were buried alive in an avalanche and the snow piled up for many years before a stretch of unusually warm winters thawed the crevasse enough that I found you under just a few inches of ice. Some friends helped me dig you out and bring you to my home. With incredible luck and certainly God's will, you breathed again with the kiss of life. I gave it to you, Noble. Please don't hold that against me."

How fragile, how strong she was, standing there with her heart in her clear blue eyes, brimming with unshed tears.

"I'd like to forgive you, but I'm not sure that I can. This is not heaven. This is not hell. You have consigned me to purgatory—a place neither here nor there."

"But you are here," she insisted. "Here with me."

Noble let go a disparaging chuckle. As long as he could laugh at his fate, then perhaps he would not disgrace himself by weeping—something he had not done since he was a boy, cowering in a closet while he watched a nightmare unfold, one even worse than this atrocity.

SIX

"Is something wrong with the soup, Noble?"

"Of course not. It's very good." He forced himself to swallow another spoonful, as he had the few others he had politely eaten. He didn't really taste it, his taste buds having gone the way of the rest of his senses. Numb.

"Here, let me warm that up for you." She took his bowl, went to a box, performed some sort of magic trick with it, and perhaps a minute later returned. "Careful, it's hot."

The rising steam seemed more a witch's brew bubbling in a kettle after the hocus-pocus Lori had worked on it. He turned his attention to the tabletop and his gaze settled on a spoon. *A spoon.* Never had he believed that something so ordinary, so blessedly familiar, would give him a sense of reassurance.

"You need to eat, Noble." Taking up the spoon, she

filled it and urged it to his lips. He gripped her wrist and raised his eyes to hers.

"Don't." He abruptly stood and said with forced calm, "I am fully capable of feeding myself, thank you. Being one of the few things I can manage without assistance, I would appreciate you not robbing me of that much self-sufficiency."

"I'm sorry. I didn't mean to insult you or—or . . ."

Noble waved away her apology and began to stalk the kitchen's length. He forced himself to confront the various oddities, proving to the lot of them, as well as himself, that he was not afraid of the strange powers they possessed.

When he pushed down a lever and began to run a finger beneath the small whirring piece of silver, Lori cried out, "Don't touch that! You'll cut yourself!" The next moment she was there, banging open a cabinet door and pulling out a can that she placed beneath the device.

"It's a can opener," she explained. "This is how it works. See?" Grabbing another can, she offered it to him with a strained smile. "Want to try it?"

In truth, he did. But not with Lori watching. He had made a fool of himself enough times this night to last him for the rest of his unnatural life.

"No. Thank you." He turned and she caught his bandaged hand. Her touch was comforting, that of a sympathetic friend. The sight of her stirred him in purely male places and would surely warm his heart if his pride allowed it.

"Look, Noble," she said, breaking the taut silence.

"I know you're confused and upset, and I can understand that—"

"Can you? Can you really understand what it's like to be stripped of everything that ever composed your existence?" Before he could stop himself, he gripped her shoulders. *"Can you?"*

With satisfaction he saw her tight swallow. Intimidating a woman, what a reprehensible thing to do, but at the moment he took comfort in exerting even this lowly show of control.

"When . . . when my husband died, I felt a lot like you might be feeling now." The sympathy in her voice was mirrored in her eyes. Tempted as he was to accept her tender offering, he clung instead to a more familiar succor: anger.

Anger he understood. It was anger, not sympathy, that he had championed against adversity.

"So, you understand, do you? How very reassuring," he replied with a mocking chuckle. "After all, how many humans could lose a loved one and liken it to being reborn in a place and time where they have no friends, no money, no home? Oh yes, dear lady, how truly fortunate I am that you understand. Because I do not understand anything except this—*I do not wish to be here.*"

She flinched at the lash of his voice, but her gaze was steady and soft. Damn her. Couldn't she at least give him anger for anger, give him that bit of a refuge to hide himself in until he could reclaim his scattered senses?

"Unfortunately, Noble, wishing won't change anything," she said gently but firmly. "You're here. I'm here. And whether you like it or not, we're in this to- gether. I'm the only friend you've got. Don't turn me away."

"Turn you away?" he sneered. "How could I possi- bly do that? After all, without you I cannot even see to my most basic of needs." Noble let go of her shoulder and flicked the front side of his pants. "I suppose that I owe you a belated thank-you for saving me from these breeches with teeth."

"I said I was sorry, didn't I? If I'd realized you'd never seen, never worked a zipper before, I would have—"

"Done it for me before I screamed for your help?" Remembering the humiliation of having Lori free him while he gritted his teeth against the pain was even worse than the lingering smarting of his flesh—minus a small thatch of hair.

"Next time you'll know how to do it yourself," she assured him. "Just like the next time you turn on the television—that is, the one I have left—"

"I will replace what I destroyed," he informed her. "I do have some bit of gold with me. Not much, but there should be ample to compensate you."

"But I don't want your money."

"No more than I want your beggar's treatment of me."

"Beg-beggar's treatment of you!"

"Call it what you wish, but I am dependent upon your goodwill." He thumped a finger to his chest. "I am a man. I take pride in being the master of my own destiny. Therefore, I can hardly call this state of breathing, and stumbling about as if I've suddenly been rendered blind, living. What you have given me is not life —it is a nightmare beyond belief."

She jabbed a finger of her own to his chest. "Do you know how lucky you are to be alive? Damn lucky. How many people cheat the grim reaper and get a second chance to enjoy all that life has to offer? Not many, Noble. Not many. And those who do usually consider themselves blessed to smell a flower again, to see a rainbow or a baby's smile. They even give thanks for the simple pleasure of tasting a hot bowl of soup."

"Have you ever considered taking to the stage?" He stared at her finger then lifted her hand and dropped it with the delicate disdain reserved for a soiled handkerchief. "Given your impassioned delivery of that moving little speech, I do believe you've missed your true calling."

He smiled. Politely. Her jaw worked back and forth. My, but he was beginning to enjoy himself. Perhaps Lori was right and he might yet be glad for this second chance at life.

"Know what? I should've left you on ice. Lord knows it wasn't any colder than you are."

"Oh yes, I agree. You absolutely should have left me there." Lightly, ever so lightly, he patted her grinding jaw. Was that a hiss he heard? He thought it was, bless her. "I believe you are beginning to understand, Lori. You see, despite your good intentions, I can offer you no gratitude for what I am not in the least grateful for."

"Should I take that to mean you'd rather be dead?"

"How very astute you are, my dear woman."

"You jerk," she seethed. "Life is a gift. How dare you spit in its face."

She snatched up his uneaten bowl of soup, marched to the sink, and dumped the contents down the drain. With a strike of her hand to the wall, a hideous gnashing sound commenced. "This is a garbage disposal!" she shouted over the noise.

She turned it off, opened a black portal, threw in the bowl, and snapped, "This is a dishwasher! I hope you were watching closely because the next time you can do it for yourself. Same thing goes for the pants, because the next time you get snagged in a zipper I sure as hell won't work it loose for you, you—you—oooohh!"

Noble savored her outburst with far more appreciation than he had her soup. It fed his need for the familiar, the revenge that flowed in his blood. It also fed his desire for this livid creature, so glorious in her wrath.

"What a provocative woman you are," he said with sincerity. "As much or even more so now as when we were in the tub. By the way, you will return me my gun now."

"Why do you want it?" she demanded with a nervous tap of her foot. "So you can kill my other television before you blow your brains out?"

He hadn't thought about that option of escape. It was viable, but he deemed suicide cowardly and a coward he was not.

The rapid flitting of emotions revealed in her transparent face captivated him, lured him to pause and study her at length. He found it admirable that her gaze never wavered from his, especially when it gave so much away. She wanted nothing to do with him. She was drawn to him against her will.

"I wish to have my gun returned because it is mine and I take comfort in the paltry possessions which I can claim as my own," Noble said quietly, with a civility he had heretofore lacked.

She sighed heavily but gave an equal measure of ground. Almost. "I'll give you the gun. But no bullets, okay?"

"It is not 'okay.' But as they say, beggars cannot be choosers, and I am done begging for so much as your pardon this night." He disliked himself for letting that last bit of poison slip out. But clearly not half as much as she disliked him for having said it.

"Fine," she said curtly as she stalked to the door. She paused long enough to say icily, "While I get your gun you can pick up your clothes in the bathroom. Consider it your first lesson in modern civilization. Women actually have lives that don't revolve around taking care of a man, and hell if I'm about to clean up after you!"

Noble silently applauded her exit. It was more than he could do for his horrid behavior. But it had served its purpose, released him from the overwhelming magnitude of what he would rather shun than confront.

Avoiding it still, he went in search of Lori's bathing room. There on the floor, his clothes were piled in a heap.

Discarded, outdated.

A burning metaphor for life as he once knew it.

SEVEN

Noble stroked his pistol in the night shadows of the bedroom Lori had said he could use for however long it took him to adjust, get a job, and fend for himself.

Though he replied that the sooner the better, he had wanted to beg her to stay, not to leave him alone with the mayhem of his thoughts. But here he was, forcing himself to face this perverse fate thrust upon him.

How would he survive? he wondered. Lori had said that people no longer rode horses in the streets, but relied on horseless carriages known as automobiles or cars. And even if he learned to use one, how could he afford the purchase? He would have to earn money somehow; yet who would employ a lawyer a century behind in his legal expertise?

Those were, he knew, the easier questions and all without ready answers. But he would learn to survive in this strange new world. Only, to what purpose? Ah, there it was, the thing he shuddered to confront. His purpose in life no longer existed, and without it, he was adrift in an amorphous sea of no meaning, with no reason for being to guide his path.

His quest for justice was gone. His thirst for revenge would never be quenched. And his vow to uphold family honor? Like so much sand in a shattered hourglass.

He felt as if he were floundering, being pulled under by dark despair. The walls seemed to close around him, and he got up, paced the room, trying the shake off this horrible sense of suffocation.

Noble touched the clothes he'd laid out to dry. Lori had offered to show him how to do it quickly by putting them in a drying machine. Though he had refused with a show of disdain for her modern contraptions, in truth he simply had not wanted to part with what little he had.

Not even the wanted poster he had found sealed to the inside of his coat and had carefully peeled away. Instinct had advised him to destroy the evidence of his crimes lest Lori find them out. Something, some fragment of memory he couldn't quite catch, warned him her reaction would be severe.

Still, he had been unable to relinquish even the poster's destructive link with his past.

By the moon's light Noble again traced the likeness of his face, the crude block lettering offering a bounty for his head. No longer soggy, the rough grain of the paper held a talismanic feel beneath his fingertips. As did the other articles he stroked, one by one.

He gathered his possessions to him, pressed his face to the worn leather and wool and sheepskin and fur.

And then he went about rearranging his things at the foot of the bed as if he were placing sacred objects on an altar.

That done, he paced some more, the crowd of his thoughts still dogging him.

"I cannot bear this a moment longer, else I'll go insane," he whispered into the shifting shadows of night.

Decisively, he made his way down the short hallway until he faced Lori's bedroom. A sliver of light bled beneath the door and onto the floor where he stood, debating.

Noble swallowed and it tasted of pride. Forcing it down, he knocked softly, twice. He heard the sound of her moving. "Yes? What is it?" she called from behind the door.

"I . . . Lori, I wondered if I might beg a moment of your time. As well as your pardon for my ill manners tonight."

"Ill?" she retorted. "That's putting it mildly."

"Yes, you're right. I was insufferably rude."

"Go on."

"And I was . . ." Lord, what else did she want? His hat in his hand? His lips to her feet? Probably. Mustering as much remorse as he could, he added, "And I was a cad."

"A cad, huh?" Was that a quiet chuckle he heard? "You forgot to mention that you were also a rake and a rogue."

"Yes, yes." He sighed. "If I add viper, villian, and knave most vile to my list of sins, will you see me?"

The door swung open and his heart quickened at the sight of her, all soft and bed-rumpled and illuminated by a muted light.

"I accept your apology—on one condition." She gave him a smile that could thaw ice and nearly torched him. "You have to accept mine for being so sharp with you. I'm afraid you hit a nerve and I let my temper get away from me."

"Rubbish. You said what you thought and what you thought was precisely true. If you don't mind my saying so, I found you stunning in your fury."

"You did?" She cocked her head, amused.

"Oh yes, absolutely. A woman has never spoken to me so forthrightly before and I was somewhat amazed by it all. A bit of the reason I deliberately urged you on."

"Why, you . . ." The purse of her lips implied he was everything he had admitted and more. "How did you bait me? Just for future reference, of course," she asked, with a hint of curiosity and good-natured humor.

"Let me see." He tapped his lips and was pleased, highly pleased, when her gaze warmed on the motion. "What I said, about you seeking the call of the theater. It is something of a questionable profession and I did acknowledge your talents in a rather mocking tone. But truthfully, I admired your impassioned speech, the flash of your eyes—even the jab of your finger. I thought you more riveting than any lead actress commanding the stage."

Lori laughed. "Who knows? Maybe I'll audition for *The Taming of the Shrew* and get cast as Kate."

"Ah, Shakespeare, the Bard most supreme. Do they still read his works in this modern age of yours?" Noble asked hopefully.

"I have a collection in my bookcase you're more than welcome to." She touched his hand and he found a sweet comfort in that small act. "His plays are still alive and well, Noble. How about we see one the next time there's a local production?"

"That would be wonderful." He kissed her fingertips. "I can't tell you how much this means to me, to know at least a few things remain the same despite the passage of time."

"Some important things last," she assured him, then added, "And other important things change."

"Such as?"

"Actors are held in high esteem these days." He nodded his approval. "And most women have enough self-esteem to speak their minds. I'm not so out of the ordinary that way." The look she gave him was one of reluctant admission.

"You think that I shall find you less extraordinary than I believe you to be once I meet other women of your time?"

"I do."

"This disturbs you," he noted, peculiarly pleased.

"Of course it does," she blurted out. Then her gaze shied from his and he thought her all the more extraordinary for her honesty despite her embarrassment. "I mean, everyone likes to think of themselves as being special. And the truth simply is, I'm not all that different from most women. I have a job so I can pay my bills and—"

"You work? You actually work away from home? This is amazing! What else do you do?"

"I shop, I max out my credit card, and screw up my checkbook balance." With a small laugh, she said, "Now *that's* amazing—considering I studied accounting before I decided to get a degree in nursing."

"You went to a school of higher learning?" Unbelievable!

"State university. I got through on a scholarship, a grant and a loan, and slinging dough at Pizza Hut. Not the easiest way to get through college, but I did it myself and I'm proud of it."

"As well you should be." Noble regarded Lori with respect bordering on awe. "What an incredible feat you have accomplished. To actually study a profession while you labored at . . . well, whatever a pizza hut is." Eagerly, then: "What else do women do differently these days?"

A mischievous smile sparked her lips. "They vote."

"Good God." Her revelations were hard even to fathom. He wanted to hear more and yet he had already heard too much. Still, he was curious as to how a woman like Lori spent her nights as well as her days.

Stealing a glance into her private chambers, Noble saw a beacon of comfort. It was a room belonging to a woman, soothing in its pastel hues, wholly feminine in its array of shapes and textures.

"Might I come in?" he asked, expecting refusal but very much hoping she would allow him to enter.

Lori silently debated. No man had come through her bedroom doors since Mick had died. She had changed it to suit her feminine whims over the passage of too many solitary years.

No need to consider a man's lack of decorating taste. No need to plot secretly the washing machine fatality of an ugly baseball cap.

The heavy, masculine furniture with dark paisley curtains and matching linens was gone, delicate white wrought iron and Battenburg lace taking its place. No, it was no longer a bedroom shared with a man, it was hers.

She did not want to be alone right now, and knew Noble did not need to be alone either. But still she asked, "If I say yes, do you promise to mind your manners?"

"I seek no seduction here, only the comfort of your company. I give you my word."

She motioned him in, struck by how small the space seemed. His powerful presence filled the room, creating an atmosphere of vivid contrasts to tantalize a woman's senses.

The vision came without warning. She saw them wrapped in moonlight and candleglow, the two of them splayed like ribbons unspooled on a bed.

The vision passed but left her shaken. Averting her gaze from where Noble stood, openly admiring her decor, she quickly went to an antique chifforobe and grabbed her favorite robe. A ratty terry-cloth ankle-hugging robe meant to give warmth to the wearer but that would put an end quick to a steamy affair.

"An interesting wrapper," Noble observed. "Is it as serviceable as it looks?"

"Uh . . . yeah." Lori suddenly wished she'd dug through her drawers for the filmy pink bit of nothing she put on when she got really depressed.

After settling herself on a white wicker rocker, she indicated he should sit too. Lori began to rock while he tested the mattress edge gingerly then fairly warmed it with his Levi's-clad behind.

Mick's jeans; so was the flannel shirt Noble wore with an uncanny air of poise and masculine elegance. It bothered her to admit it, but Noble looked better in Mick's clothes than Mick ever had. She resented Noble a little for that—but not half as much as she resented herself for noticing.

"So, what's on your mind?" she prompted.

"Too much and more than I can sort through. I sought you out with the hope you might give me some advice."

"I have a better idea. You talk and I'll listen."

"You're sure you don't mind? The hour is quite late and I do tend to pontificate when caught up in a debate —even if it is internal."

The bedside clock said 3:00 A.M. and she had been due to punch in at seven. Had been. Once she'd said her less than hospitable good night to Noble, she'd called in sick. Talk about an acting job, she'd wheezed and coughed out her excuses for the two days she was certain it would take to shake her sudden flu. Two days wasn't much, but even mad as she had been, she'd known she had to help him get his bearings and catch a breather herself before confiding in Ryan.

She wasn't angry anymore, but felt just a little—okay, a lot—uncomfortable with the cozy, exciting sensation Noble's nearness provoked. "Forget the time," she told him. "We can sleep in late. So go ahead, spill your guts and pontificate away."

"Very well, then. I am terribly distraught," he confessed. "Nothing is familiar here and I'm given to wonder if I will ever claim that simple luxury of feeling normal again. Not only with my surroundings, but here." He pressed his palm to his chest, near his heart. "Within."

"Some things in life never change, Noble. The search for inner peace is as old as time."

"Yes, and small consolation that is." He fell silent and studied his hands as if he were a palm reader searching for a nonexistent lifeline.

Lori quit rocking. She wondered so much about this man who was an enigma wrapped in a riddle. But compassion overrode curiosity. "Were you at peace with yourself in your past life?" she asked.

"No. But I had made my peace with the path I was compelled to follow. That path is denied me now and I am left without a sense of direction. I feel so hollow inside, Lori, as if I'm a stranger to myself."

"I know how that feels and it's not a good feeling."

"It's terrible," he whispered. "My life has traversed many twists and turns but never have I lost sight of the purpose which guided me."

"And what was your purpose?"

"A worthy one." He left it at that. "It is gone now as if it never existed."

"But you exist," she reminded him.

"Do I?" He looked at her then, a scrutinizing stare. "My endless dreams seemed real, as real as this moment we're sharing now. It leaves me to wonder if this is the dream and I shall awaken in the place you stole me from. How can I know, Lori? How can I know what is real and what is not? For certain, there is far more unreality about me here than from where I came."

Leaving her chair, she went to him, put her arm around him, and gave him a hug.

"Hugs are real, Noble." She grasped his hand and squeezed. "So is holding hands with a friend who cares. You are real. I'm real. Believe it."

"I don't want to. But . . . I do. Lori," he said in a hushed, confidential whisper, "please don't think less of me for confessing this, but I am afraid."

"Think less of you?" she repeated, incredulous. "Good Lord, Noble, do you actually think it makes you less of a person to admit being afraid?"

"Of course. To show fear is the sign of a weakling. At least for a man it is."

"But it's okay for a woman to be afraid, right?"

"Certainly. And it is a man's duty to protect her from whatever or whomever she is frightened of."

Lori considered setting Noble straight on his antiquated ideas in the role-playing department. Better saved for later, she decided, when he wasn't so upset.

"Look, Noble, being afraid does *not* make you a weakling. It makes you human. In fact, if you weren't afraid of what you're dealing with now, I would question your sanity."

"You would?" At her nod, he said in a rush, "Thank you for easing my mind on that score. Quite frankly, fearing for my sanity was part of the reason I came to your chambers."

"Whatever the reason, I'm glad you did, I'm glad we made up and more than glad to tell you that no way, no how, are you crazy. And now that we've got that straightened out . . ."

"You wish me to leave?"

"No, I wish you to stay." Even as she said it Lori had to wonder if *she* was insane. "At least for a little longer. You see, I have a problem of my own. I've got—"

"Insomnia." He looked as surprised by his insight as she. But then he pressed his temples, concentrating, and said, "Ever since your husband died, you've had trouble sleeping."

Lori was momentarily speechless. "How did you know?" she finally said.

"I'm not really sure. I just . . . knew." Noble's perplexed expression gave way to one of such absolute connection that she felt as if they were linked by an indelible bond of empathy. "Tell me, Lori. When you were a little girl, did you really jump from a roof, thinking you could fly?"

"I was six. I broke my leg." Stunned and disconcerted, she wondered how much had he absorbed in his deep-sleep state. "Do you remember anything else I told you about myself?"

He thought for a while, then shook his head. "Bits and pieces, but very little comes together to make any sense."

Lori sighed her relief while a part of her was somewhat disappointed. The idea of Noble knowing just about everything there was to know about her held a certain appeal.

Still holding hands, she felt his thumb stroke hers.

"Something does come to me now. It was about how your husband died—not naturally, some sort of tragedy. Will you tell me again?" When she hesitated, he added, "I'm almost as good a listener awake as I am asleep."

"Okay," she slowly agreed. "Mick was a policeman and he was gunned down in a bank robbery." A soft groan came from Noble and she saw distress cloud his face. "You look upset."

"I—" He took a deep breath and let it out on another groan. "Yes, this upsets me. Greatly. Had I known —remembered—I . . ." He grimaced. "I wouldn't have been so beastly about demanding the return of my gun."

"That's okay. Really, it is. These are threatening surroundings for you—and besides, you come from a time when most men kept their guns as close to their hips as they would their wallets these days."

"You're very gracious, Lori. More than I deserve," he said with a thread of humbleness she didn't understand. No matter, it plucked at her heartstrings anyway.

Hands touching, their gazes connected, Lori

deemed him an exceptionally sensitive man, even by current standards.

"Do you wish to tell me more?" he asked her, his voice oddly strained.

Maybe if she did, just maybe she could sleep for a change. And maybe if she did, Noble would feel free to unburden himself to her. She sensed that something was troubling him, deeply, something beyond his obvious turmoil.

No doubt it was rooted in his past, perhaps sprang from those secrets he had mentioned in the tub. But any man who thought being afraid made him a sissy wouldn't easily part with his secrets or his darker demons within.

Whatever they were, she couldn't imagine them being any darker than her own.

EIGHT

"I was on duty at the hospital when it happened. Mick was rushed into the emergency room and he was so—so covered with blood that I didn't know who it was at first. But he was still alive and I heard him call my name while all these other people tried to drag me away from this—this man I loved who was calling for me."

Lori . . . sweet . . . heart. I'm sorry . . . so . . . sorry. She heard his voice again, so clear she could remember the shallow wheeze of his breath, the gurgling sound in his throat as he began to asphyxiate on . . . blood. *So much blood.*

Struggling for breath herself, she whispered, "I could hear him only because I was clinging to the stretcher, kissing him—I was kissing Mick and telling him that I loved him and everything would be all right. I told him that I wouldn't let him die, that I'd never forgive him if he did. And then—and then . . . He died." Tears welling in her eyes, she stared hard at Noble. "Know what? I still haven't forgiven him. It's too much to forgive."

"God," Noble breathed out. "Dear God."

"I haven't forgiven Him either." Knuckling tears from her cheeks, she said too brightly, "So, there you have it. My very own passion play, filled with murder and angst, a high drama worthy of the stage. Hey, even Shakespeare couldn't have done better if he'd written the script himself."

Her mirthless laughter fell like brittle chips of ice in the too still room. But then she felt his gentle fingertips push back her hair, his warm breath beside her ear.

"Might I hold you?" She shook her head and pulled slightly away. "Why not?" Noble asked.

"Be-because I'm afraid I'll come apart if you do."

"Would that be so bad?"

"Oh yes, bad." Chancing a glance at him, she was rocked by the soul-deep compassion in his gaze. She felt herself teeter on the verge of throwing herself into his arms, begging him to make it all go away, to render her numb to everything except for the magic of his touch.

"Very bad," she reiterated with more force.

"I don't understand."

"It's really simple, Noble. I'm a lot like Humpty-Dumpty. I had a great fall, and I've done my best to put myself back together again, but some pieces are missing. So it's really important for me to protect myself from anyone or anything that might jar what I've managed to keep intact."

"But if you would let me, I would like to help you find those missing pieces so you might be whole again."

Lori considered his offer. She needed some help and Lord knew her counseling sessions and grief group hadn't gotten her over the hurdle she continued to straddle—on better days.

Thinking aloud, she said, "It's strange, but I actually do feel better since I told you about it—again. I don't talk about my real feelings to anyone, not in the last couple of years anyway. Not even to my parents or my friends. Hell, I don't even talk to myself about them anymore, my feelings just keep me awake, when I'd sell my soul for a good night's sleep. And here we are, not really knowing each other, while I spill my guts all over the place like you're the best friend I've got."

"Nothing would make me happier than for that to be true." Noble tapped his lips, those marvelous lips that tugged at the corners and made her slightly smile too. "I feel a bond with you as well, Lori, one which defies logic and time. I pray that we shall always be the best of friends. Friends . . . and more."

He looked as though he wanted to say more than he was actually saying. Or maybe it was just her, projecting onto him all the contradictions that defined her life and never got resolved. When would she get beyond the past and get on with her future? And yet, in the short time Noble had been with her, she had taken some great strides forward.

Did she dare take another? A small but significant step that would alter their already unique relationship. Perhaps it was that uniqueness that was imbuing her with the courage to take the risk of listening to her heart, not her head.

"I'd like you to do something, Noble. Something I haven't let another man do in a very long time." Reaching for the bedside lamp, she switched it off. "Hold me? And more."

"How much more?" he murmured, taking her into his arms.

"I don't know yet." How solid, how natural and good she felt in his easy embrace. "For now, I just want you to hold me until I go to sleep." She rubbed her cheek against the coarse stubble of his. "This feels right."

"It *is* right."

Even as he said it Noble knew it was not right at all. Something terrible was between them, something he could not ignore. Neither could he ignore her fleet kisses to his check, as they shifted downward on the bed. He pulled the covers over them then urged her head to his chest.

Lori nuzzled against him, stroked her palm over his heart. It beat too quickly, too heavily. For her. Hold her, she'd asked. And hold her he would, forever and beyond if she would but let him. But just as he had stolen back his gold, he was stealing these precious moments now. This Noble knew.

Her husband stood between them—more surely than the fabric separating their bodies as her knee slid between his.

Noble's breath caught while her own became even and deep. In sleep she sought a natural fit, Lori's covered thigh wedged against his groin, pressed like a secret promise against the strain of his arousal.

It was a sweet torture Noble endured, listening to her breathe, smelling her apple-scented hair, stroking it while he imagined stroking into her with a gentle fury—an imagining that made his body ache where she pressed.

Yes, he was hurting there; but even more he was aching in places unseen.

Early dawn turned the white shades of the window a pale lemon. The room softly illuminated, he shifted his gaze to the bedstand and stared grimly at the picture he had avoided looking at since he'd first entered her room.

Encased in a silver frame was a lifelike image of Lori in a wedding gown, her face radiant as she smiled up at a formally dressed man who could only be Mick.

A handsome chap, though a bit long in the jaw.

Noble's own jaw tightened.

Mick wasn't dead, not really. Even from the grave he had a powerful hold over Lori's affections. And her loyalty. Noble could understand that, having lost his parents much the same way. Nevertheless, he considered this man, this Mick, his enemy.

Not only must I compete with your exalted memory, he silently told him, *your martyrdom has put me in a dreadful position.*

His eyes narrowed in hostility at the picture, Noble carefully reached over and turned it down.

He gathered Lori more tightly to him. Her soft sigh made him yearn to sip the breath from her lips, tautened his keen need for release. Release, how he did need it. A borrowed escape from the mire of his troubled thoughts, some small ease for his physical distress, which she worsened with her nuzzles.

Never had he felt such comfort and discomfort all at once. Never had he sought ease in the arms of a slumbering woman, but he held Lori as if she were his own, not the lawman's.

The man whose ghost stood between them.

Lori stretched languorously as she came slowly awake. Ahhh . . . mmmm, but she felt so rested, so at peace, so—

She sat up with a start. Bright light beat against the window shades and she knew it must be midday. Had she overslept? Impossible, she never overslept. A quick glance at the bedside clock informed her that the impossible had happened.

About to bound from the bed, Lori stopped.

"Wait a minute. . . ." she whispered. The cobwebs clearing from her head, she felt surging images from the night before rush in, wave upon wave.

Her gaze went to the pillow that bore proof Noble had been there. A single rose lay where his head had been. Beside the rose was a note. Lori picked it up and was struck by the elaborate flourish of his handwriting, a stark contrast to the pharmaceutical-company heading on her notepad—the one she kept beside the kitchen phone. An uneasy premonition niggled at her, but she pushed it aside and proceeded to read:

My dear, Lori, I took the liberty of plucking a flower from your garden, for it reminded me of you—yellow petals the color of sunshine. Fragile and soft, belying a strong stem and the threat of thorns.

Lifting the rose, Lori ran a fingertip over the stem. And smiled. The thorns had been removed.

While strolling your front grounds, I saw many things which pricked my curiosity—even more so than the oddity in your kitchen which allows voices to speak, some in foreign tongues even, with a random press of numbered buttons.

Lori's groan gave way to a gasp of alarm.

Should you awaken before I return, no need to fret. I have gone to embark upon what promises to be a grand adventure but shall return in time to take tea with you. Quite an assortment I found in your pantry—as intriguing and delightful to the senses as you, my lady.

Faithfully, I am yours—Noble

"Oh my God," she breathed. "Oh my God!"

Leaping from the bed, Lori tossed aside both flower and note and took off, shouting, "Noble! Noble! Are you here? Please, be here!"

His room, maybe he was in his room. No Noble there. Just a made-up bed and Mick's pants folded neatly at the end. By the time she flew into the kitchen, her heart was pounding, her stomach churning, and her imagination racing faster than her feet. *Oh Lord, please don't let him get run over or arrested or taken to the psych ward at the hospital.*

She had to find him before someone else found him first. The more help she could get, the better. Ryan, she'd call Ryan at work, then Warren, Jacob, and Jennifer, and tell them to beg off from their jobs, too, on account of an emergency.

Grabbing the phone, she fleetingly wondered where in the world Noble had called. No time to worry about it now, she'd worry after she got her phone bill.

Just as a ring sounded on the other end, the doorbell buzzed.

Maybe it was Noble. Maybe he'd locked himself out and was back, safe and sound. If he was, she'd cover him with kisses and hug him like she'd never let him go. And then . . . then *she'd kill him*.

"Emergency room. Hello . . . hello?"

Lori slammed down the phone and rushed to the front door.

She threw it open and sighed her relief.

Relief that lasted all of two seconds. Next to Noble stood a man in uniform.

"Uh . . . hi. Hi, Jack! Long time no see."

"Good to see you, too, Lori. Sorry to wake you up, but . . ." He turned his attention from her—disheveled and bed-rumpled, she realized, and quickly pulled together her gaping robe—to Noble, who bowed slightly in her direction.

"This man says he's a friend of yours, Lori. Is that true?" Jack gave her an apologetic smile, letting her know he didn't believe it for a minute. "I picked him up walking down the middle of your street—got a call on him from the local pawnshop. Seems your 'friend' here tried to buy a television with a pouch of gold."

Lori summoned what she hoped passed for a burst of laughter.

"Noble," she said with a roll of her eyes while she latched on to his arm and all but yanked him inside. "I know you have this crazy thing about getting into your characters, but actually pretending this is the gold rush . . ." She sighed dramatically. "Really, Noble, this is too much."

"You mean, you actually know this guy?"

"Of course I do," she said, hooking her arm around Noble's shoulders—*stay away from his neck or you'll strangle him*—giving the appearance that they were the best of buds. "Noble's an old friend from college. Just visiting, taking a break from Hollywood while he gets into his part. It—it's one of those shoot-'em-up frontier-adventure flicks."

"Hey, no kidding?" Jack got a starstruck look in his eyes as he regarded Noble. "A real live Hollywood actor right here in Juneau! Have I seen you in anything before?"

"Probably," Lori interjected. "He's done a lot of bit parts, but this is his first major role. Noble takes his work very seriously. In fact, I'm almost surprised he didn't rent a horse and take to the streets on it. Fortunately, he stopped with the wardrobe and a pouch of fake gold."

"Might I have my gold back, please?" Noble drew himself up and extended his hand.

Jack gripped it. "Well, I'll be damned. A real, live Hollywood actor with a lead role and I'm shaking his hand! Sorry about making you sit in the back of the squad car. I thought you were maybe a loony tune from the psych ward who'd met Lori and got some crazy ideas," Jack said while pumping Noble's hand.

"My gold, please," Noble repeated, unsmiling.

With a lopsided grin, Jack handed it over. Withdrawing a pinch of it, Noble offered it to him. "I'd like to pay you for taking me in your . . . car. I very much enjoyed the ride."

Jack shook his head and flipped out his citation pad.

"Think I could have your autograph? If you're half as good on screen as you are off, you're gonna hit it big. Especially with the ladies. Anyone ever tell you that you kinda look like Clint Eastwood?"

"All the time," Lori said. Noble shot her a narrow glance as he signed his name with a flourish.

"There you are, my good man."

"Wow, sounds like you've got stage experience too. Were you ever on Broadway?"

"I performed in England. Shakespeare."

"Man, wait till the wife hears about this. Great to meet you, Noble."

"A pleasure, to be sure."

"Thanks, Jack," Lori said, feeling ignored.

"Nooo problem. Take 'er easy, Lori." Jack turned to leave and she exhaled a deep breath. But then he called back, "By the way, what's the name of the movie you're in?"

The question was directed to Noble. She whispered, "Tell him it's called *The Gold and the Glory*."

Without looking at her, Noble replied, "It's called *Guns and Roses*." With a gracious smile, he added, "See you at the, ah, movies, Jack."

NINE

"Tea?" Noble asked, pulling out two cups and scanning for matching saucers, which he slid from the bottom of a pile in the cupboard.

"Fine." Lori drummed her fingertips on the table.

"You're sure you don't mind me rummaging about your kitchen?" After her muttered, "Fine," he filled a kettle with water and took it to the stove. Paused. Given the magnitude of what he had learned on his own in a few short hours, surely he could master this rudimentary skill without her tutoring.

Noble studied the placement of knobs, their relation to the four black circles. He settled the kettle on one then selected the lowest setting. By the time the steam whistled, he had prepared the tray, as well as himself, for what was bound to prove a less-than-genteel tête-à-tête over tea.

After pouring the boiling water, he turned the stove off. Amazing that he should take pride in such a minor accomplishment. But he did. Just as he took pride in having come to realize one did not walk in the middle of the street. While horses and carriages paid proper respect to those who took to their feet, automobiles apparently did not.

Automobiles. Otherwise referred to as cars. What an exciting invention. He couldn't wait to master the driving of one himself. Driving, not riding. This he had gleaned from Jack, a jolly good chap—even if he was a lawman.

Looking over the assortment of boxes, he selected the one he deemed most appropriate for Lori.

"Would you care for Red Zinger?"

"Fine."

He placed the tea bag into her cup then chose Earl Grey for himself. While the tea steeped and she continued to drum her fingers, Noble set out two plates, a tube of crackers, and a brightly labeled jar of peanut butter. It was the best he could do given the sparseness of her pantry contents—which he had investigated hours ago, as he had much else in this house filled with infinite wonders.

"Sugar?"

"Fine."

Unable to resist, Noble ladled four heaping spoonfuls into her cup. He usually took one for himself, but certain he was due far more tartness than sweetness from Lori, he added an extra sugar to his own tea.

"Cream?" When she didn't answer, he filled the remainder of her cup with a generous splash. "Have you any cognac?" he asked hopefully.

"Cognac?" she repeated, looking at him directly for the first time since Jack had left. "All I've got around here is a six-pack of Bud Light and two bottles of André, fermenting in the fridge since New Year's Eve. Oh yeah, and a bottle of Crown Royal I bought for Mick. An anniversary present for an anniversary that didn't happen."

Crown Royal. The liquor's name appealed to Noble. Not so the reason for Lori's having bought it.

"Never mind the cognac. Have you a cheroot laying about you might spare me?"

"Smoking's bad for you. It can take years off your life."

"Given that I've bought more years than most people can possibly imagine, what's the loss of a year or even a dozen. More to the point, why do you measure life in years rather than experience? To eat, laugh, and dream to your heart's content without censor, that is life. And to fill your pipe while you consider all of this, it is a pleasure to indulge in. And without pleasure, what is life?"

She stared at him for a while, then shook her head and muttered, "The hell if I know." She went to a drawer and searched through it. She lifted two cigars, one brown, one wrapped in pink foil. Stalking back to the table, she tossed the former to him, along with a small box of matches and an ashtray. She peeled the wrapper off the cigar she kept for herself and began to lick what appeared to be chocolate.

"Life's weird, you know? I mean, why do people pass out cancer sticks to celebrate a new life?"

Though he did not know what cancer had to do with cheroots, Noble grasped the gist of her quandary.

"Life and death," he observed, "have much in common." He bit off the cigar's end, lit it with several light puffs, and inhaled what proved to be . . . acceptable.

"I never thought so before," she said tightly, "but I can definitely see the connection now."

Watching her suck on the phallic-shaped chocolate, Noble felt a twinge in his groin. Could it be, he wondered, that respectable women of this day might indulge a man with such intimate acts as those that had once been the domain of harlots? While his pants tightened uncomfortably Lori took a sudden bite off the end. His wince coincided with her shout.

"Dammit, Noble! Don't you ever pull something like that again or I'll—I'll—"

"Kill me?" He blew a smoke ring then sipped at his too sweet tea. "Oh, come now, Lori, there was no harm done."

"No harm done? The hell! You scared the living daylights out of me. And then—then! My stomach's still twisted in knots from lying through my teeth when I can't lie worth a damn. But you? You didn't even break a sweat, acted like the whole thing was no big deal. But it was. It was a big deal, Noble. *Read my lips.* It was a big deal."

"Please, calm yourself. Drink your tea."

"I have no intention of calming myself!" She slapped the table so hard their cups rattled. "Do you have any idea how crazy I went when you took off and left me screaming through the house, praying that you were safe while you wandered the streets without me?"

"Clearly, I was far safer without you while I found my way about alone than I am in the presence of your company." Spearing her with a level glare, he charged, "I may be living in a time where I don't belong, but I am not stupid. I learn quickly, Lori. Know, therefore, you need never answer for me again."

Grabbing her cup, she took a gulp—and gagged. "This is awful," she choked out.

"Then perhaps the next time I ask you how you take your tea, you'll give me a better reply than 'fine.'" He tapped his ashes while she silently seethed.

"Guns and Roses?" she suddenly said with a fake bit of laughter. "Next time try to come up with something more original, okay?"

"Personally, I like it. However, since you don't, the next time you seek to put words in my mouth, make them more original than *The Gold and the Glory.* How bourgeois."

"How bourgeois," she mimicked. "Tell me something, Noble. Why the hell do you have the last name of a Russian and talk like a Brit with a broomstick up his butt? Excuse me, up his aristocratic derriere."

"Derriere. That's French." He raised a lofty brow.

"If you'll notice, I'm not laughing. Look," she told him seriously, "if you're going to live in my house, I have a right to know something about you."

"Such as?" he returned smoothly while his guard rose.

"Such as where you picked up all your polish that

doesn't jive with the mean streak you've got running a mile wide and just as deep. And don't tell me you don't have one. I saw it clear as day last night. And I don't like that 'Who me? I'm innocent' look on your face one bit when I know full well you're no innocent when it comes to the uglier side of life." She gave him a scrutinizing look.

Had she found the wanted poster he'd hidden beneath the mattress of his bed? Noble consoled himself with the certainty that Lori would have tossed him out onto the streets she wanted to protect him from had she discovered it.

"Should I choose not to oblige you, will you send me on my way?" Even if she did, he could survive. But he did need Lori, in more ways than he had ever needed another woman before; and so, yes, he would allow her to know him as few people ever had—after she gave him the answer he wanted.

"No." With a heavy sigh, she said again, "No. I won't make you leave, but I'd feel a lot better if I had some kind of idea about who you really are. Besides, it's only fair. After all, I told you about what's happened in my life. You can't blame me for wanting the same from you."

"Very well." He caught a glimpse of the rise of her breasts as she leaned eagerly forward, and remembered how soft they had felt against his chest, how hard she made him now with her hair a mess and face washed clean of the makeup she didn't need. "However, since divulging such matters is a rarity for me, I'm inclined to attach a price to the telling of my story." With his gaze fixed on her mouth, he named his terms.

"I'll have a kiss in exchange. Payable upon demand."

The tip of her tongue fleetingly brushed her bottom lip, sorely tempting him to demand his kiss then and there.

"All right," she slowly agreed. "A fair exchange."

Deciding to savor the anticipation of kissing her—and oh how deeply, how slowly, he would kiss her—Noble braced himself against the emotions he could feel gathering like a hard fist twisting inside his chest.

Exercising a steely control, he said quietly, "I was and always will be a man who is what he is. Imperfect but proud and self-sufficient. Certainly able to care for himself and provide for those who are reliant upon him."

"I've learned not to rely on anyone but myself," Lori was a bit too quick to assert.

"Oh?" His regard was a deliberate reminder of the night before when she had needed him to hold her. In her eyes he saw a flash of vulnerability. It made his own more acceptable. "Such lessons are hard ones, Lori. As it was with you, my life was once graced with the security of loved ones and many wonderful privileges. I took them for granted, of course, until they were gone."

She touched his hand as he stubbed out his cigar with more force than was necessary. "What happened?" she prompted.

"In the end, something quite terrible. But I'll get to that later. For now I'll explain the circumstances of my rather unique lineage. My father was a poor, distant cousin to the czar, but was held in very fond regard. He was given a large parcel of land here, some years before Seward committed his great folly by buying this godforsaken land in . . . what was it? Oh yes, 1867. Anyway, my father deemed it better to remain amongst uncivilized people than to return to his homeland where he would be titled but penniless. Here, at least, he might strike gold and return to Russia a rich man."

"Did he? Did your father find gold?"

"He did. Several years later in a mountain's cave on his granted estate. He was wise enough to keep the discovery to himself, but decided to hell with living like a pauper in the middle of nowhere. He didn't dare leave for long, but he did set out to indulge himself with a visit to San Francisco, where he quickly spent his gold on fine vodka, fine living, and a particularly fine lady. My mother. She was the daughter of an English aristocrat on holiday with her family."

"Wow," Lori breathed. "It sounds so romantic."

"I suppose that it was. But not entirely. You see, despite my father's own title and newfound wealth, my mother's parents were highly opposed to the liaison. They insisted she return to England and marry posthaste the proper suitor she was engaged to. Defying them, she secretly married my father and ran away with him to Alaska. By the time Mother's family found her, living in a rude shelter—Juneau wasn't even a tent city yet—she was with child. Me. Her father disowned her. He left with a shattered jaw, compliments of *my* father."

"Whew. That must have been one doozy of a fight."

"Yes. Needless to say, when I found my way to my

grandfather's doorstep, he was less than gracious in his welcome to 'the Russian's bastard' as he so fondly referred to me. I was around the age of ten at the time."

"What a horrible thing to say to a child!"

He likened Lori's outrage to that of Attu. Attu, who had saved his life, seen him to safety in England rather than the much closer realm of Russia. No living grandparents, uncles, or aunts were there. Just distant cousins who would surely have shown more compassion than the grandfather and an assortment of relations in London, the lot of them proving about as warm as a winter drizzle shrouded in fog.

Noble let go a single, harsh laugh. "Ah well, I've gotten ahead of myself. This being a distasteful chapter in the book of my life, I'll get it over and done with swiftly. Prior to throwing myself on my grandfather's untender mercies, I had enjoyed a good life. My father built his wife and son the grandest house possible on our land. He saw to it that we had servants—Aleutians —and an imported tutor so I might have a proper education. Of course he couldn't do all this without it becoming apparent that he had struck a rich vein of gold. Consequently, we lived with the threat of attack."

"Is that how you ended up at your grandfather's?"

Noble gave a curt nod and wished fiercely for the cognac.

"Will you tell me about it?" she asked gently.

"Regretfully, Lori, I cannot. Perhaps another time, but for now suffice it to say . . . what I witnessed was a waking nightmare. It was a miracle that I escaped butchery myself—a miracle I have Attu to thank for. He was more than my personal servant, Attu was my mentor and most trusted friend. It grieves me, wondering what became of him, whether he lived into old age and prospered or suffered an unkind fate."

Lori nodded in understanding. "If you'd like, we can go to the library and see if there are any old newspapers, maybe try to find out that way."

He would go, Noble determined. But it had to be a private search, lest some details about his crimes emerged in antiquated print, linking him to Attu. Dear Attu, who may very well have lost his life because of him.

"I think it better not to know." A lie but a necessary one. "I'd rather imagine the best than discover the worst and be powerless to champion him should he have met a dire end."

"I'm sorry, so sorry I had to be the one to tell you about him being gone." Her eyes glistened with the tears Noble longed to cry himself for Attu's loss. But he had learned not to cry long ago, the value of "keeping a stiff upper lip" beat into him by his grandfather, who had wielded an unerringly cruel cane.

"And I am glad it was you who told me. As difficult as this transition has been for me, it could not have been much easier for you. I cringe whenever I think of how badly I took the shock. Actually turning my gun on you and calling you a demon of the dark—" Recalling it, he shuddered. "I am truly sorry for that. But just as it was with the overtaking of my family's land, what is done is done. The best one can do is get on with living and come to terms with what cannot be reversed, as best one can."

"The uneasy peace," she whispered, sliding her fingers between his and clasping his hand. "You said you'd made yours with the path you were compelled to follow. I'd really like to know what that path was, Noble."

He would tell her a bit of it, but not all. Not until he earned her trust and won her heart so completely, even his past crimes could not tear them apart. Lori's heart, yes, that was what he wanted. To win it was a purpose more pure than and just as worthy as the one he had lost.

"The road was long," he said crisply, "and anything but straight and narrow. I was a rather wayward youth, giving my grandfather the worst grief I could. I preferred untitled friends to titled; dallied with, shall we say, women who were splendidly raucous, when, in truth, I was secretly taken with the ways of more gentle-born ladies, who possessed those traits I had so admired in my mother. All the while I did my best to do poorly in school. But in the end I proved myself quite capable in the study of law. Much to my grandfather's delight. He was, after all, a member of Parliament—"

"Parliament!"

"Ah, so you're impressed."

"Of course I am. Who wouldn't be?"

"Me." Noble smiled at the memory. "I took my greatest revenge on the old man by refusing to accept his offer to groom me for an appointment myself. Instead, I left the esteemed practice where I had been employed and returned, with Attu, to Juneau. By then I was well into my twenties and certain of my ability to see justice done with the silver saber of my tongue. Alas, I was mistaken. My attempts to bring to trial those men, who were rich, having laid claim to my rightful land, were laughed at. They fairly ran me out on a rail."

"That's terrible," Lori breathed. "Worse than terrible. It's about the most unfair thing I've ever heard in my life."

"I couldn't agree more." Though she supported his feelings, he doubted she would support the means by which he had sought his ultimate justice. He might get sympathy, but it was empathy he was after. His own for Lori was great. Much of what he'd unconsciously absorbed, the unguarded whole of her life, was coming back to him.

He'd been granted a rare privilege, and he honored it with a respectful silence. The whole of his life he kept silent as well, respecting the choices he had made while he longed for the day he could divulge them to Lori.

This was not the day.

"What happened after that?" she pressed, her voice a mixture of compassion and curiosity.

Carefully, he answered, "Attu and I took up residence in Skagway. Though it was dangerous, I did return to Juneau a few times, but always at night and incognito."

"So that's why you were so concerned about your whereabouts at first." At his nod, she frowned, puzzled. "Okay, now I understand what you meant about me keeping your secrets safe and it explains you having two identities. But what I don't get is why you'd risk coming back to Juneau when you had enemies here."

"It's really quite simple, my dear." He leaned close. "Pride. Not to return would have been an admission of defeat. And of cowardice. I am no more a coward than I am a quitter. Or a fool. Hence, the precaution of disguise and the gun I'd learned to shoot rather well, a better protection than law books could provide.

"So there you have it, Lori," Noble concluded. "And now that I am done telling my tale, I will exact my price for it." He watched as she nervously wet her lips, which whetted his appetite to consume them with a fury.

Noble swept aside their cups and gripped the lapel of her robe. A small jerk and he traced her lips with his tongue.

"My kiss, Lori. I would have that kiss from you now."

"O-okay," she stammered. "But just a kiss. That's all."

Noble laughed softly. "Could it be you might actually have as much to learn from me as I have to learn from you?"

"No doubt," she answered, her breath coming shallow and fast. "But what does that have to do with a kiss?"

"Only everything, my dear." He nipped her bottom lip. "I've yet to well and truly kiss you. Though I daresay, once I do, you'll realize any real kiss from me will never be 'just a kiss.' "

TEN

Lori glanced at the clock: 2:00 A.M. She tossed and turned another half hour before slinging aside the covers. While she paced she worried her still-swollen lips.

Damn Noble. Damn him anyway. By no stretch of the imagination was that a kiss he'd given her. Kisses stayed on the lips and even involved one tongue getting turned on by another. But a kiss did not include a man's slow and deliberate roving over a woman's neck, ears, and the cleavage he exposed with his teeth to the bodice of her nightgown.

Lori wiped her forehead. Sweating, she was still sweating. But surely any woman would be sweating for days after a kiss that gave new meaning to extended foreplay—only, if Noble considered *that* a kiss, what in heaven's name did he consider foreplay?

Lori felt her knees go weak, her inner thighs quiver just wondering. And remembering. Remembering how he'd pressed her down on the table, her protests a sequence of moans as she'd pulled him on top of her. And there she'd writhed among peanut butter and crunched the crackers with her back, not even realizing what she was doing until Noble drew away.

He'd left her there on the table, speechless, as she watched him pick up the mess on the floor. That done, he had gone to the refrigerator, taken out a variety of vegetables and a package of chicken.

And then in the most polite tone he had informed her, "In exchange for your hospitality, I'll assume a variety of tasks. Actually, I'm a fairly decent cook—a matter of survival, since I never took a wife." When she simply stared at him, he came to her and pulled her robe together. "No need for you to linger, I can find my way about without assistance. Once dinner is prepared, I'll call you to join me," he said with a gracious smile.

She left, still searching for words that wouldn't come.

By the time he rang a bell—a leftover from Christmas she'd never gotten around to storing with her mishmash of ornaments—her tongue still refused to function. His own, however, appeared to be in fine shape. Over a candlelight dinner, her best china set out on the tablecloth she used for special occasions, he had glibly related several stories about the misadventures of his youth, interrupted only by his questions of concern.

"You don't care for the salad? Ah, I see, the salad is fine but you prefer 'Diet Ranch' over vinegar and oil. . . . Is there something wrong with the dinner? Too many onions, too little gravy . . . Neither, is it? Then why don't you eat what I prepared? Not hungry, you say? We'll see about that. Voilà! I saved the best for last. Behold, dessert."

She had stared at the bowl he set before her, two big scoops of vanilla ice cream with swirls of chocolate running down the sides, crushed nuts sprinkled over the top. She watched while he dug into his dessert, barely touching her own.

While he busied himself cleaning the kitchen she had stalked to her bedroom. And now here it was, over six hours later, and she was still stewing, wanting more than anything to ravage Noble's mouth with a vengeance. The thought of waking him up was mighty appealing. After all, if she couldn't sleep, why should he—

Suddenly Lori heard a familiar sound. Distant, but unmistakably there. Fighting a grin, she managed a scowl and marched to the living room.

"What the hell do you think you're doing?" she yelled.

Continuing to slide the vaccum with one hand while he cupped his ear with the other, Noble shouted back, "Pardon me? I can't hear what you're saying."

Lori jerked out the plug. "What I'm saying is that you woke me up."

"My apologies. I couldn't sleep, you see, and while busying myself about the house, I happened upon this sucking broom. I was so taken with it—"

"Why couldn't you sleep?" Misery liking company, she could only hope Noble's reasons were similar to her own.

He shrugged. "I fear once I do, I might slumber for another century before waking up."

"Not likely. After all, you're safe and sound in a house, not camping out on a glacier."

"What you say is true, very true. But still, the apprehension lingers."

Lori sympathized more than she wanted to. She told herself to send Noble to bed and go to her own—*alone* —once she did. But that's not what came out of her mouth as she tugged at his arm and said, "C'mon, let's go to sleep."

"I would if I could. But I can't. For several hours I tried. Now off to bed with you. I'll cease my noisy sweeping and leave you in peace. Oh, have you a feather duster about?"

Lori groaned. "A neat freak. If you're a neat freak, I can tell you right now that we're not going to get along," she informed him, her hands on her hips.

"A neat freak?" he repeated.

"Yeah, one of those people who can't get a life beyond their obsession with flicking the dust from a white glove that's glued to their hand."

Noble looked at his hands. "No white gloves here. And a bit of dust never bothered me. I was only seeking to distract myself from a troubling perplexity."

"And just what's troubling you?"

"You."

"Me?"

"But of course. I made dinner for you in the hope that I might gain your appreciation for more than my ability to kiss. And what did my efforts get me? Silence. Silence from you, other than a few cursory responses.

And you didn't even grant me the courtesy of a single word after I kissed you."

"Did it maybe, just maybe, occur to you I didn't know what to say after—after . . . I still don't know what to call it. You called it a kiss. That was no kiss, Noble."

"It most certainly was. Though admittedly, I did not relegate my exploration to your mouth."

"That's putting it mildly," she huffed. "And as for me not saying anything, what about you? Puttering around the kitchen, acting as if nothing had happened, while I tried to pick myself up off the table. Do you know how that made me feel? Used. Discarded. You hurt me, Noble."

"Oh, no." He blew out a heavy sigh and laid his palms on her shoulders. "I would never deliberately subject you to such feelings as those—please, you must believe me. It's just . . . I thought you might wish for some distance while you put yourself back together, so to speak. And perhaps I thought this because it was my own need." Searching her eyes, he explained, "Lori, I've never been so deeply affected by a woman before. When I let you go, I wasn't sure what to do with myself —with the state of my emotions. And the obvious other." He slid his hands down her arms, cupped her hips.

His groin flush with hers, he said, "The obvious other, Lori. Had I not left you to collect some self-control, I very well may have committed a dishonorable act. You deserve better from me, good and decent woman that you are. And no decent man would bed such a lady until he had taken her to wife. I regret my show of respect caused you distress, when it was my way of relaying my feelings for you. Deep feelings, Lori. They are not common or shallow." He rubbed slightly against her. "Neither is my body's response to you."

Her own body's response was immediate and intense, quickening and moistening with the rigid feel of him pressed to where she was soft and aching. But it was more than his body doing this to her. It was Noble himself, an extraordinary man with a code of honor outside her experience. And of any other contemporary woman, she was sure. They'd be after him in droves once he was on his own. Maybe before.

Already she resented her faceless competition. Already she could feel her heart break as she imagined the moment when they parted. As they would. It was inevitable.

And it was that inevitability that caused her to hug him tight, press her cheek to his chest so he wouldn't see the keen passion, the distress in her eyes.

"You're a wonderful cook, Noble," she said quietly. "Almost as good a cook as you are a kisser."

He crooked a finger beneath her chin, urged her face up.

"It takes two to truly kiss. I admit to having my share of experience at it, but never have I felt so thoroughly kissed back by a woman as I did by you."

How much longer would she have him to kiss? she wondered. She didn't want to think about it. She couldn't stand to think about it. All she wanted to think about was that for now Noble was hers and she wouldn't waste a minute of this specialness they shared for as long as she could have it.

"Will you sleep with me again tonight?" she whispered. "Hold me like you did before? You don't have to stay, just as long as it takes me to nod off and maybe dream." Oh, the dreams she'd had last night. No nightmares of Mick bathed in blood for the first time since he'd died. She'd dreamed of Noble, the two of them finding an easy peace together as they made love. Wild and uninhibited lovemaking and more.

"Would you grant me another kiss if I agree?"

"If I agree to that, I'll never go to sleep. But since I'm really, really tired . . . make you a deal. Lend me your chest to sleep on, and once I wake up you can have a kiss—after I brush my teeth."

Noble's low, seductive laughter sent tingles from the roots of her hair to the soles of her feet.

"I propose a more fair bargain," he said with a shrewd smile. "I'll share your bed and your covers, but it is my turn to have you for a pillow." His gaze dropped to her breasts. "A much softer pillow than I could ever provide for you."

"Sounds fair to me," Lori replied. Better than fair, it sounded wonderful. In all the world there was nothing quite like holding and being held by a man resting his head against a woman's beating heart.

Lori took Noble's hand and led the way to her bedroom. Only, somehow, he was soon leading her. Once there, Noble took off her robe, pulled back the covers, then motioned her in. He didn't immediately join her.

Standing by the side of the bed, he held her motionless with a steady gaze while he undid the buttons of his shirt.

"I'll leave it on as well as the breeches," he said, pulling the tails from his pants.

"If you want to take off your shirt, I've got no problem with that." *Please, take it off.*

There was something odd about his hesitation, the flicker of indecision she glimpsed before he shook his head.

"I'll leave it. A bow to your virtue, if you will." With his chest exposed, but the shirt left on, Noble's reluctant gallantry rang more false than true.

"How do you—or did you—usually sleep?" Lori asked before she could stop herself.

"For as long as I can remember, I've preferred a crisp, clean sheet against my bare skin. Even when it's cold out beyond belief, I'll take an extra blanket before wearing a nightshirt. So tell me, what of yourself? Do you always wear a long gown and a serviceable wrapper to bed?"

Again, Lori wished for the filmy pink bit of nothing in her drawer. "Just the gown—lately, that is. Before Mick came along, I slept in a T-shirt. Then, once we started sleeping together, I wore nightgowns. And then I quit wearing those. But after he died, I started wearing nightgowns again. I don't know why."

Why was Noble frowning? she wondered. She rushed on to say, "What Mick and I had together was good. Right and good. From the first time he touched me, I knew he was the man I had been waiting for. I didn't have to think twice about agreeing to marry him, sleep with him for the rest of our lives—or, as it turned out, the rest of his life."

Noble's brow furrowed. "Forgive me if I'm mistaken, but were you actually intimate before pledging your vows?"

"Of course we were. Almost all couples are before they get married these days. In fact, some women have several lovers before they settle on one."

"Might I ask how many you've had yourself?"

It wasn't anyone's business but her own, but since he'd asked nicely, with more curiosity than machismo, Lori answered him. "So far, Noble, I've had one. At least if lots of hanky-panky in the backseat of a car doesn't count. Now, turnabout being fair play, what about you?"

For a second she actually thought he was too stunned by her question to respond.

"I, ah . . . suffice it to say, I've had more intimate partners than you. However, none of them for very long. Once I returned to Alaska, I occasionally sought the favors of harlots—not to be confused with courtesans, who take pride in their illustrious trade." He laughed, ruefully. "But why should any man need the services of either, what with feminine sensibilities as modern as your own?"

"Believe it or not, my sensibilities aren't modern by a long shot compared with plenty of others." Had she told him that because it was true—which it was—or was it because a part of her wanted to stay on the pedestal Noble had put her on? Both, she decided, and hastened to add, "I'm not into recreational sex—never was, never will be. I'm just not made that way."

"Yes, I know." A slight smile, a probing gaze, and he asked, "How are you made, Lori?"

"Like everyone else, from a certain mold but different from anyone besides myself. When I commit, I'm in for the long haul, Noble. I'll take the laughter, the fights, the sex, the tears, and be happy with that. Even if a relationship went sour, I could never cheat."

"This I believe. And yet why do I have the uneasy sense you feel as if you're cheating on your deceased husband by keeping company with me?" Noble narrowed his gaze on the wedding portrait beside the bed.

Lori wanted to tell him what he said was ridiculous. But she couldn't. There was a part of her that most definitely felt like she was cheating. It was the same feeling she'd struggled with in the tub and come to terms with. But now here it was again, resurfacing and intruding on what she wanted, desperately needed, with another man. It made her angry with herself, resentful of the memories that wouldn't let go. *She had to let them go.*

With a silent prayer for forgiveness, Lori reached for the picture. Hand unsteady, determined, she turned it down.

Noble flipped up the wedding portrait, the moment frozen in time, staring them both in the face.

"I will sleep with you, Lori. But I will not now, nor will I ever, be a part of your guilt. Your reasons for wanting to shut out your past are far different from mine for wishing to do away with it. You do not wish

Mick to see you with me—that is it, isn't it? After all, you are still bound to a man who resides in a picture beside your bed and in your heart. Can you deny it?"

More than anything, she wanted to. Fiercely. In Noble's eyes she saw a silent plea that she would. But what he'd said was true and she couldn't lie to him any more than she could to herself. Sadly, Lori shook her head.

"Your bed is too crowded for me." Noble refastened a button at his waist. "When there is room for me, and me alone, to lie beside you, let me know. Until then . . . sleep well."

He turned to leave.

"Wait." Lori was off the bed and gripping his arm before she gave herself time to hide in the safety of cowardice. Her gaze veered from him to Mick's memory. Meeting the challenge, she said, insisted, "Sleep with me. Now."

"Just with you?"

"Just with me. You and me, nobody and nothing else."

"Prove it."

It wasn't Noble she had to convince beyond simply welcoming him into her arms. It was herself that demanded more substantial proof that she had confronted and conquered this thing she could not allow to keep consuming her life.

Lori stepped back until she came even with the bedstand. Slowly, deliberately, she released the top button of her nightgown. And as she did she stared at her wedding picture, the couple who no longer existed outside a silver frame.

Her hands were unsteady, but still, she released the second button. It was painful to make herself do this, the difficulty of her actions intense. But so was the liberation Lori embraced.

This was different from coming apart at the seams in a tub or on a table, when she hadn't known what she was really doing. But what she did now, what she was compelled to do, was for herself more than for Noble. For herself more than for him, she stared at the past while baring herself to another man.

Lori drew aside the bodice of her gown. She lifted out a single breast. And as she did it she wept. Eyes open, she wept in sorrow and in joy as she turned her gaze to Noble, letting him see so much more than the nakedness of her breast.

Noble could not blink. He could not speak. What he saw moved him as he had never been moved before. A single breast, a beautiful, full breast was all Lori had revealed. And yet she had exposed her very bones, her soul. He could love this woman. As he stared at her, amazed by her depth and courage, he wondered if perhaps he didn't love her already.

He watched her as she cupped her palm beneath the pale, rounded weight and in silence offered it to him.

"Dear God," he breathed. "Dear God."

"Sleep with me," she whispered again.

He bent his head, bowed before this remarkable woman, a lady beyond measure by any standards, and laid his cheek to her breast. As he did Noble reached for the lamp.

They fell onto the bed and embraced beneath the

covers, his chest pressed to hers, their cheeks just as close. He whispered into her ear what he'd never said to a woman before. That she was both angel and demon, capable of possessing his very soul. That she gave him a sense of unrivaled peace even as she robbed him of what little peace he'd ever claimed in life, past or present. He told her that he didn't dare kiss her because if he did, he wouldn't be able to stop.

Lori said nothing, nothing at all to his confessions; yet she spoke volumes when she urged his head down.

His need was dire to fill his mouth, suckle her ever so gently and with a passionate fury. Noble did neither.

Whatever the standards of this time were, they were not his. And if ever there was a woman worthy of his protection, his vows of faithfulness and provision before reaping her favors in bed, it was Lori.

The woman he would take for a wife.

His senses filled with the beat of her heart, the feel of her fingertips stroking his hair, he held her ever so tightly until she stroked no more and her breathing was even and slow.

Only then did Noble allow himself to steal a taste, just a small taste, of her breast.

It tasted of home.

His last conscious thought was that he did indeed love Lori. And sleep though he might, he would not well and truly rest until her past and his were like so much fodder sparking a flame that would not, could not, die.

ELEVEN

"You're sure you'll be okay?" Lori asked.

Noble reluctantly tore his gaze from the television and assured her, again, "I'll be perfectly fine. Just as I promised, I won't wander the streets or play with the telephone. Neither will I attempt to pet the dog next door since he has a tendency to bite. As for your car, no need to worry I'll attempt to drive it since you're taking it to work."

Beep, beep! Beep, beep! Returning his attention to the animated character Lori had said was a cartoon, Noble said distractedly, "By the way, thank you for treating me to that marvelous ride out yesterday. The only thing I enjoyed more than exploring the supermarket and the dry-goods store was the driving lesson you gave me."

Beep, beep! Beep, beep! The Roadrunner sounded much like the automobile's horn. He felt a thrill at the prospect of toying with the assortment of dashboard gadgets again.

Watching the silly coyote fiddle with a box of gadgetry and blow himself up, Noble slapped his knee and burst out laughing. Glancing up, he noticed that Lori wasn't even smiling as she tapped a white shoe.

A rather unattractive one—almost as ugly as that atrocious wrapper she had a habit of wearing about the house. Taking her in, he felt his loins quicken. The short white dress and matching hosiery clinging from slender ankles to just above shapely knees more than compensated for her other attire.

"If it's not too much to ask, could you drag yourself away from that stupid cartoon long enough to kiss me good-bye?"

In a few long strides he met her toe-to-toe. Narrowing his gaze on her mouth, he said, "Am I to understand that part of my household duties include kissing you on demand?"

"Well . . . yeah."

"I'm not accustomed to being ordered about," he informed her with mock severity. "I am, however, quite comfortable in placing orders of my own." He slid his arm around her waist, bent her backward, and demanded in a hot whisper, "Kiss me." When he was done, Lori staggered back, her lipstick smudged from the bottom of her nose to the end of her chin.

She checked her watch. "Oh great," she gasped out. "Now I'm going to be late."

"Then you'd best hurry along—before I make you even later than you already are." Noble licked a finger and rubbed at the lipstick on her chin. "When you come home, all will be as it should be. Trust me."

"Okay. But remember, call me if you need anything. I left the number beside the phone and—"

"Yes, yes." The sooner she left, the sooner he could make use of the phone and set his plan for independence into motion. Shooing her out, he said, "God-speed."

She squared her shoulders and turned away.

"Oh, Lori," he called down the hall.

"Yes?" she asked expectantly.

"You still have lipstick on your nose."

He chuckled as he heard her retreating grumbles, soon followed by the sound of her car squealing out from the driveway. Then, returning his attention to the television, he laughed even harder as he watched the Roadrunner outsmart his nemesis yet again.

"Lori? Lori. Oh Lorreee, anybody in there?"

"Huh?" She looked up from the chart, and it took a few seconds for reality to register. "Oh, Ryan. Hi."

"Are you still sick? I was worried about you when I stopped by after work yesterday and you weren't home, even more so when you didn't answer your phone later. But strange as you've been acting this morning, I'm getting concerned as hell. You've been clocked out ever since you clocked in."

Lori debated, then motioned him into the empty break room. Closing the door, she took a deep breath and said in a hush, "He's alive, Ryan."

Ryan snickered. "Sure he is, Lori. Sure he is. Now,

if you'll excuse me, I'll be right back with a head doctor."

"No, Ryan, I mean it. He's really, really alive. His name is Noble Zhivago and he's got the most incredible past. Get this—his father was a cousin to the czar, who gave him ten thousand acres of land and—"

"Whoa." Ryan held up his hands. "Are you actually telling me that the amazing human Popsicle—"

"Don't call him that," she snapped. "His name is Noble and he's a wonderful, fascinating man."

"I don't believe this." Ryan shook his head as if trying to wake up after a wild night out on the town.

"Believe it. He's already adapting, and too fast to suit me. At the rate he's going, I'll be lucky to have a couple of months before he's on his own. But till then, he's mine."

Ryan considered her at length. "You're really crazy about this guy, aren't you?"

"Something like that," she admitted.

"So, when can I meet him?"

Lori hesitated. She had to let her friends meet him sometime, and she wasn't worried about Noble holding his own. What did worry her was the possessiveness she felt. Jennifer she trusted, but that didn't hold true for some other gal pals, who'd pose a threat once they wrangled an introduction. Suddenly the Kick and Kaboodle seemed more a place to avoid than not.

"Tell you what. I'll check it out with Noble and see what he thinks. Maybe you can join us for tea—"

"Tea!" Ryan hooted.

"Yes, *tea*. Feel free to bring along a few cheroots—"

"Cheroots?"

"Cigars, whatever. Just don't bring along anyone else."

"Not even Martha?"

"Especially not Martha." Gal pal number one she did not trust. "And don't say anything to Jennifer. I want to talk to her about the situation before she meets him."

"My, but you're sounding territorial." His knowing smile mingled with a look of brotherly concern. "Set up the tea and I'll bring the cigars."

"If you really want to impress him, throw in a lighter."

"Sure, Lori. But I can tell you right now, if he doesn't impress me as the kind of man who'll be good to you, then I'll light into him faster than he can flick his Bic."

It was just past noon, and what a full day it had already been. A deeply disturbing one, Noble thought. His trek to the library had been for naught, a scavenger hunt through the archives for some small news of Attu that did not exist.

He would never know what had become of his beloved friend, and despite what he'd said to Lori, not knowing was immeasurably worse than an eternity of wondering. The only relief he could claim was finding no mention of himself in the sparse assortment of aged newspaper clippings.

With a troubled sigh, Noble tapped the phone. No

relief there for a certainty. He'd made the necessary calls to determine his options and obstacles before plotting his course of action. Limited options; obstacles aplenty.

How amazing it was to learn so much in so little time. Unbelievable really, how much one could discover from simply pretending to be a writer doing research for a novel. Equally astonishing was that the university professor hadn't laughed at what surely seemed to be a ludicrous idea.

He'd said he was working on the story of a lawyer who went to sleep for a hundred years and awoke, here, in present-day Juneau. Amid adventure and drama and seeking to win the hand of his lady fair, he determines to restore his credentials. *How* would he do it?

Quite good-naturedly, the professor had said there was no school of law in Alaska to attend and brush up on his skills, but there was a state law library. One was conveniently located in Juneau. If the character in question had proof of having graduated from an accredited law school—even if he'd earned his degree a century prior—then he could take the state bar and, once he passed, hang out his shingle again.

Simple enough. And yet, not simple at all.

Noble knew he had been blessed with keen mental abilities and tutoring himself would present no problem. As for producing a certificate of graduation, there was a slender chance he could acquire a copy. Yet another phone call to an English operator had netted him the number to his alma mater. Cambridge was still in existence.

The problem lay in convincing the necessary individuals he was indeed in existence himself. And should he manage to do that, then he would be confronted with the biggest problem of all. Lori had been adamant, urgent, in her warning that his true identity must remain secret. She had told him the consequences would be severe, that he would endure public scrutiny, even perhaps be taken away for study by all manner of curious experts. She had said it would not matter to them that he was a person, entitled to a private life or—

The phone rang and Noble jumped, automatically reaching for his holster. Gone. Of course, he reminded himself, men did not wear their guns about these days.

He felt a pang of longing for the time to which he belonged. But no, here he stood, listening to the phone ring and following Lori's instructions to let the answering machine do the speaking. This did not sit well with him, not well at all. Pretending to be invisible while Lori's life marched on.

"Noble? Noble, are you there? It's me, Lori. If you're there, pick up the phone."

He did and said, "Yes?"

"Just checking on you. Is everything all right?"

No, everything was *not* all right. "All is well, Lori. How fares your day?" he answered.

"I miss you," she whispered.

"Good," he replied crisply. "Once I'm done with the laundry, I'll begin dinner. Have you a request?"

"Something low in calories and high on taste. Say, conversation for dinner and kisses served up with hugs for dessert?" She laughed softly.

Noble eyed the table and suppressed a groan. He could drink forever and beyond of their conversations, which never ran dry. And Lori's kisses, they were so sweet and delicious, they left him starving for more. But he couldn't have more, not until he found a way to provide for her. It was a matter of honor, of pride.

"Since man does not live by bread alone," he said, lifting a towel to check the dough he had rising on the countertop, "you may have kisses for dessert."

"Can't wait. Which pretty much sums up how a friend of mine feels about meeting you. I told him if it was okay with you, he could join us for tea on my next day off."

Him? "Certainly. Has *he* a name?"

"His name is Ryan. We work together."

"I see." Indeed he did. While he played house-keeper Lori went off to work and spent her days with Ryan.

"You'll like him, I promise. Ryan's a really great guy. He was with me when I found you. We're climbing partners," she went on to explain. "I told him I was hanging up the ropes for a little while. Ryan said he understood, even though he was jealous since I'd rather spend my time with my new roomie instead of with him and his coffee."

She laughed as if it were an incredibly funny joke—but Noble found no humor in it. A roomie, was he? And as for this "really great guy" who did more than work with Lori . . .

Noble jabbed a finger into the dough, pretending it was Ryan's throat.

"Then tea it is. Make the arrangements and I'll see to its execution." Executed. Though he wasn't dangling from a rope, a hanging might be a pleasant respite compared with this. This twisting in his gut. This terrible jealousy he'd never experienced before. This pleasant exchange of good-byes when he wanted to pour out his frustration and misery as if he were a child, not a man.

Noble sank the rising dough with a crushing blow of his fist. He did not like the bread bought from stores. Again he slammed down his fist. He did not like being relegated to baking bread while Lori went to work. With Ryan. *Pound. Pound.* He did not like playing the role of a "roomie" who slept, merely slept, with a woman he longed to take for his own, to share all manner of intimacies with.

Pound. Pound. Pound.

When the dough was flattened to the thinness of unleavened bread, he kneaded it with angry, vicious swipes, then, with supreme control, returned it to its former shape, covered it with a kitchen towel, and stalked to the laundry room.

He folded Lori's sweaters and small denim pants. Whoever heard of a woman wearing pants? Though he couldn't deny the way Lori wore them deserved no less than accolades.

She wore her pants well.

Too well. He admired her independence almost as much as he resented it, feeling more and more as if he were bound in a corset and skirts.

Yesterday's adventure had indeed been grand; however, there were a few events that had bothered him.

Lori had taken him shopping and bought him clothes, seen him to a barber and helped him choose the cut of his hair. But afterward, she had taken him to a jeweler and . . .

Noble smiled smugly. He had interceded when she fumbled for an excuse to explain why he would possess a pouch of gold dust. It was not so far from the truth, his story of coming into this peculiar inheritance from a great-grandfather who hadn't trusted banks.

The gold was exchanged for a bank draft, and he and Lori had been at odds as to its placement. She had wanted to deposit it into her account for safekeeping since he lacked the necessary papers to open an account for himself. To hell with that! After some heated debate she had cashed the bank draft—which he'd had the foresight to request be made out in her name—and once they returned to the car, she'd thrust the bulging envelope at him with a curt, "Here."

He had counted the greenbacks. Not because he didn't trust Lori, but because he had no faith in banks, and yes, two thousand five hundred twenty-two dollars was there.

Despite her resistance, he had reimbursed her for the clothes and barbershop visit she had paid for. So, too, he insisted on compensating her for his destruction of what he'd learned was called a "big-screen TV." Grudgingly she had named the price of a hundred dollars to call them even.

He'd laid five times that in her lap. Did she think him so dim-witted that he couldn't read a newspaper advertisement? He would repay the remainder of his damages once he was gainfully employed, he had tersely informed her. And what money he kept would go toward paying his way until then.

Laundry piled from waist to chin, Noble stomped to her bedroom. Jerking out a deep drawer, he shoved in her things. Then he went to check the pummeled dough. It was not fully risen, but he was impatient with more than the baking of bread. He returned to her room and confronted his nemesis.

Grabbing the framed wedding picture, he snarled, "Damn you, Mick. Damn you for dying as you did. As if I don't have enough to deal with, I have to wonder, constantly wonder, will Lori ever love me enough not to loathe me when she learns of my crimes." He put the frame down with a sharp thud and tried to comfort himself with the knowledge that no one but he could tell her of his lawless acts.

Little comfort there. Deceiving those deserving of his honesty, his fealty, did not sit well with him.

Lori deserved his fealty and more.

He paced her bedroom, filling himself with her presence as he moved among her things. At the vanity he looked into the mirror encased by carved wood. "You will tell her. You must. But first you will win her heart so completely, she shan't be able take it back, no matter how direly she might long to," he said to his scowling image.

Not wanting to look at himself any longer, at the distress he didn't want to see, could not let Lori see, Noble picked up a silver-handled brush.

He touched the soft bristles, the softer strands of her

hair. Pulling one out, he rubbed it between his fingers and knew a fierce want to tangle his hands in her hair, press his palms against her temples as if he could squeeze out those memories of his deceased rival.

Yes, his rival still. Perhaps Lori had begun to let Mick go, but he was not yet able. Mick had claimed her for his wife. Mick had made love to her. And Mick had provided for her in a way he himself could not.

Not unless he took the bar exam. Not unless he subjected them both to the same horrendous public scrutiny he had witnessed on the television and in newspapers at the grocery store.

If only he could reclaim his hidden riches—

Noble sucked in his breath. Why had he not thought of this before? Any true outlaw would think first and foremost of his stolen wealth, even if he'd slept a hundred years and come back to life. Then again, he wasn't a true outlaw. And Lori did have a way of distracting him.

Adrenaline surging, he tried to calm himself with the numbing bite of reason. Had Attu escaped an untimely demise, while his partner in crime had not, then he would have claimed the gold that had been marked for purchase of the land they had sworn to share.

But if, *if*, the gold still remained, then he might buy back his rightful holdings after all—nearly a century later. To think of it, just to think of having that wonderful, embittered piece of his life returned, to share it with Lori, was to believe the past might yet grant him some justice.

Making a rapid translation of the money from the

jeweler exchanged for his pouch of gold, Noble put his hidden worth at approximately a million in modern currency.

With hope, his heart leaped.

Just as quickly it fell.

How would he explain to Lori his newfound wealth? *Bloody hell.* Even if he could borrow her car while she slept and go to the cave tonight, the gold would do him no good. No amount of riches would do him any good if he lost her in the process. Time. Yes, time. He must be patient.

His mind worked swiftly, forming a workable plan. He would find a way to visit the law library regularly and absorb legal information as quickly as he was able— in case the gold was gone, which quite possibly it was. If such was the case, he would be prepared to take the bar, a worthy risk in exchange for his ability to assume the role of husband and provider. Meanwhile he would continue with his domestic duties and woo Lori with passion and with purpose.

Passion. Noble groaned, long and deep. *Long and deep.* It was how he yearned to take her as she slept in his hungry arms. Restraining himself was becoming increasingly difficult. Perhaps they should no longer sleep together. Lori trusted him, but he trusted himself less and less. A battle waged inside him even now as he laid down the brush and hesitated only slightly before opening a shallow vanity drawer. It was an invasion of her privacy, but still, here he was lifting a pair of dainty panties, fingering the lacy band.

Lori wasn't even in them and he felt a surging response as he stroked the thin silk. Feeling himself grow so hard that he ached, Noble vowed that this was the closest he would get between her thighs until his wedding ring graced her hand.

Vows were meant to be kept at all costs, not broken. And yet this was one vow he questioned. Clearly, it was outdated, but then again, so was he. Lori, however, was not.

She was such a modern woman, he could scarce believe she viewed herself as being somewhat out of step with the times. How could she possibly think that? The array of scanty underthings he now sifted through were anything but prudish.

"Noble! I'm ho-ome!"

Her distant call of his name had him shoving the panties he still held into her drawer and slamming it shut.

"Noble? Noble, where are you?" Lori called again.

"Here!" he shouted. With no apparent evidence of his small transgression, he automatically grabbed the first innocuous thing his hand came in contact with.

"Oh, there you are." She rushed into his arms. "I'm so glad to see you. How'd it go today?"

"Fine, perfectly fine," he said with a strained smile.

"Brushing your hair?" She gestured to the brush he held.

"Actually, no. I was considering how to go about asking you if I might brush yours." Good, very good. Delivered with the convincing innocence of a lawyer who knew in his heart the person he was protecting was guilty as sin.

"I'd like you to brush my hair," she murmured.

"Before or after dinner?" he asked, trying very hard not to think about the raging instincts gone amok in the privacy of his pants.

"Both," she answered in a throaty whisper, swishing her hair over her shoulders.

Noble laid aside the brush and stroked his fingers through her fair, golden hair. So beautiful, so fine, the feel of her so right, he suddenly knew that no matter his current ability to provide, no matter the human perplexities defining this time, he could not bide this much longer.

Sniffing, she said, "Something sure smells good."

"It could be me."

"Could be and is," she assured him. "But I could swear that's fresh bread I'm smelling." She licked her lips. "I know it's too good to be true, but did you actually use that yeast we bought yesterday? As in, stirring it up with some flour and whatever else it takes to bake a loaf of bread?"

"I did." Much as he deplored this maid duty, Noble took pride in having done some small feat that Lori had yet to accomplish herself.

"Home-baked bread." She sighed. "Forget the diet margarine. I've got a stick of real butter."

"Two sticks remaining. I took inventory. And while I was at it I noticed that your two bottles of André bear the denomination of champagne."

"Cheap stuff, but it's okay." She laughed self-consciously. "There went the mood. Just goes to show how out of practice I am when it comes to romance."

"Quite the contrary," Noble told her, "I find your candor refreshing." He bit softly at her earlobe, tugged a small gold hoop with his teeth. "I also find it *very* romantic."

"Noble," she whispered. "Noble, what am I going to do with you?" She paused, sighed sadly. "And once you're gone, what will I do without you?"

"A moot question since you won't be rid of me until you throw me out. As for your immediate concern . . . have me for dinner. And should you find yourself still hungry, have me again for dessert."

Noble pulled away and studied her glowing face. As he looked at her now his multitude of dilemmas slid away.

"You make me feel so rich, Lori. Even richer than a land baron discovering a wealth of gold in his mine."

"Know what? You make me feel like gold."

"You are," he assured her. Indeed, Lori was gold. A woman of immense strength and vulnerability. A woman he would be very foolish to let go for any reason.

Breaking away, she dug into her purse and extended a book. "From me to you. Louis L'Amour. He's kind of like the Shakespeare of frontier fiction."

"Thank you, Lori—and now a gift to you in return." Noble traced the novel's binding down her spine, tossed the book away, and caressed her behind.

Angling for a kiss, he tossed away his principles as well. And judging from her rampant response as he palmed a warm, full breast, there was much to be said for wooing a modern woman minus one's old-world principles.

TWELVE

She had come to a decision. A very important, life-altering decision. But as Noble studied her too incisively while she swallowed a generous sip of pink champagne, Lori was no longer sure if she could act on it.

She finished the glass and he refilled it, his darkly sensual gaze never leaving her overwarm face. A cool compress sounded good. So did some deep-breathing exercises alone in the bathroom while she reconsidered the wisdom of what no longer seemed necessarily wise.

Seducing Noble. What in the world had made her think she could pull off something so outrageously brazen? *Fear and courage. Desperation and desire.* Yes, that's exactly what it was. She feared losing him; she was desperate to keep him. But facts were facts and the simple fact was, for all of Noble's professed affection and steamy kisses, she was his first stepping-stone into the future, and once he got his footing, it would be only natural for him to expand his horizons beyond her and their relationship.

It wouldn't be long before her monopoly on Noble was history. She had realized that today, when she'd let Ryan enter the picture. And that's when she had determined to seize the moment, to be brave enough, foolish enough, to see to her needs without worrying about tomorrow.

The problem was, her needs went beyond desire, and already she was worried about picking up the pieces of her heart once Noble was on his own. Later, she told herself, worry later and quit wasting precious time, and while you're at it quit shaking your foot and say something—something provocative.

"This is delicious." Delicious as it was, the bread felt stuck in her throat and she washed it down with several long swallows of champagne. "Where did you learn to make bread?"

Noble shrugged. "A simple task, really. Simple enough for a boy to learn from watching cooks in the kitchen."

The hot silver gleam of his gaze on her wet lips had Lori reaching for the bottle. Noble caught her wrist. His fingers seemed to burn past her flesh and into her jumping pulse.

"Please, allow me." Again he filled her glass, his actions smooth and polished, unlike the faint shake of the glass as she lifted it. "Is something wrong, Lori? You seem not quite yourself tonight."

Maybe she should just tell him. Just tell him she was terrified he would break her heart. And once she spilled her guts about that, ask him if he'd mind seducing her since she had no experience in seducing a man.

But . . . no. *No.* She was a grown woman and fully capable of taking charge of her life, taking responsibility for her actions.

"Actually, Noble, you're right. I'm not quite myself." Lori put down the glass and squared her shoulders. "I came to a decision today. And once I did, I went shopping. On my lunch hour. Alone."

"It sounds as if your decision was a monumental one, given the message on your—what is it called? Ah yes, bumper sticker. 'When the Going Gets Tough, the Tough Go Shopping.' " He chuckled. "So, tell me, what sent you to the stores?"

"You. Me. I mean, us." Lori groaned. This wasn't coming out right. Maybe she should have written him a letter instead. Too late for that; she plunged on. "What it comes down to is that I want to keep you all to myself, but all I have is borrowed time. Today is today, tomorrow is tomorrow and—"

"Lori—"

"No, Noble. Let me finish. I've resigned myself to the cold, hard facts. Even if you break my heart, it's not worth giving up a single minute of what we can have now. And so, I went shopping. First, I bought a really sexy nightgown. And then I bought—" A box of condoms. She couldn't bring herself to be so blunt. "I, uh, picked up a bottle of cognac, some vanilla-scented candles, and threw in a box of Trojans. I meant to light the candles to set the mood before I slipped into my new nightie and wave the cognac at you while I drew you down on the bed."

Lori blew out a sigh of relief, glad to have gotten it all out into the open and thankful Noble hadn't laughed at her. Far from it, he looked aroused and intrigued.

He took a leisurely sip from his nearly untouched first glass of champagne, lifted a brow, and asked, "What are these Trojans in a box?"

"They're—they're . . ." Oh Lord. Why hadn't she just gone on the pill? *Because by the time they kick in, the affair might very well be over.* She took a deep breath. "They are thin plastic shields a man puts on to prevent pregnancy and protect both partners from sharing any sexual diseases." At his expression of slight offense, Lori hastened to say, "Not that I have any because I don't. And I'm sure that you don't either. But it's the responsible thing to do."

He tapped his lips. "Amazing that you could and would actually purchase these . . . ah . . . French letters"—he paused—"in order to prevent a chance taking of my seed I presume."

"That pretty well sums it up."

"Should I take this to mean you don't wish for children?"

"No! I'd love to have kids."

"How many?"

"Heck, I don't know. Two? Three, max."

"An acceptable number." After a thoughtful silence, he quietly added, "I look forward to the day when those French letters are no longer of use to us."

Wasn't he listening to her? Obviously no better than she was listening to her heart before it was shattered.

"We can't even think about a family, Noble. For heaven's sake, we can't even think about being together beyond tonight and a few stolen tomorrows. That's why I'm trying to drag you to bed—so far, with little success —and no wonder since I—"

"Enough." He slammed down his glass. "Enough of this skirting around the real issue. It is not that I will break your heart by deserting you, because I have an equal fear you will desert me. The true difficulty lies in that I am absolutely, unapologetically in love with you, I will be for the rest of my life, and I shall have you for a wife. However, I cannot ask for your hand until I am financially sound again—and though I vowed to myself to honor your virtue until I'd earned the privilege of claiming it, I simply can't wait that long before seeking your most intimate favors in bed."

For a full minute Lori could only stare at him. "Let me get this straight," she said slowly. "Are you telling me that you think you're in love with me?"

"I do not think it. I know it. Just as I know my father fell in love with my mother in less than a week as well. I've dallied with many women, in bed and out, but never has one laid me low and sent me soaring, with a smile, a kiss."

How she wanted him to love her and how easily, too easily, it would be to love Noble. He made her feel too much, want too much. And there was the danger.

Hard as it was, she clung to reason. "There's a big

difference between the two of us and your parents. They came from the same time—"

"They also came from two very different worlds. Love is love, they often told me, no matter the poor timing of it or the adversity which might come as a result." He took her hand, pressed his lips to it. "I do love you, Lori."

"Tell me that in a year and I'll believe you."

"I will. Time will prove I speak the truth. And time will prove whether or not you can return the love I freely give to you. Tell me, do you feel some, even a little, now?"

Did she? Heaven help her, but she did. All the more reason to make him understand the distance she was compelled to keep. "I'm crazy about you, Noble," she confessed. "But I don't want to let myself love you the way you think you love me. I can't afford it. Not yet. Not until you—"

"Meet other women of your time?" he supplied. "Back to that, are we? Bloody hell, woman. Not only do you underestimate me, you underestimate yourself!"

"I'd rather underestimate us both than end up in love with you only for you to figure out what you're really feeling is something a lot less." Before he could refute her, Lori touched his hand. "Look, you need me to help you get through a painful transition. And I need you for the same reason. Please, Noble, why don't we just agree to leave love out of the equation? That way you won't feel guilty if you decide to leave and I won't be hanging my hopes on a shooting star sure to burn out when it hits ground."

Noble suppressed a disdainful retort. *Leave love out of the equation, eh?* For not having known Lori long, he seemed to know her better than she knew herself. She wasn't capable of shutting off her emotions while coupling. He would refrain, however, from righting her misguided reasoning. Especially since it abetted his cause.

"Very well," he agreed. With satisfaction he noted her slight frown at his seemingly easy capitulation. He twirled a fingertip in his glass and traced a wet path from her throat to the scooped neckline of her blouse. Dipping inside, he leisurely flicked a nipple. At her soft gasp, he withdrew. "Very well," he repeated. "If it is a lover you want, a lover I shall be. A demanding one, Lori."

She wet her lips, a nervous little gesture. "I—uh, I'll go put on my nightgown. While I do, you can—"

"Watch. You are sorely mistaken if you think to relegate me to cleaning the table or pacing the floor while you do battle with the decision you've made."

She stood with stoic resolve. Noble admired her courage even as he shook his head at her resigned sigh. "Okay. Let's forget the dishes and—"

"And be done with it?" He blocked her way when she took a halting step toward the stairs. Staying her with a firm grip, he felt her slight shake. Lord, he thought, if Lori only knew how painfully revealing his own disrobing would be, she'd surely realize her anxiety had nothing on his.

He spoke to himself, as much as to her. "To take off one's clothes, Lori, is to bare your body but not necessarily your soul. No one can see or touch that part of another unless it is given freely, with trust. I trust you as I have few others, and will gladly bare myself, body and soul, for your view. However, I need at least some small measure of the same from you." Searching her troubled, yearning gaze, he felt an incisive empathy with Lori, as if he were in her skin, not his.

It had been like this since he first awoke, but the more time that passed, the more his sense of connection with her intensified as her unguarded revelations surfaced in his memory. How well he understood Lori. Even her present reluctance, her need to be loved by him and her fear to believe it was true. Somehow he had to break past her defenses and win her trust. But . . . how?

As he thought his gaze veered to the table and the second loaf of bread, untouched, covered by a towel. Lori was like the waiting loaf, its steam held in by external forces. And he was the knife capable of cleaving her defenses if she would but lend her hand to the cause.

"Lori," he said, breaking the charged silence, "what do you say to my need for more than just sex? Surely you realize it won't be good for either of us unless intimacy is part of what we share."

Noble was right. Lori knew he was absolutely right. Without intimacy, she'd feel cheap and empty. But once she lowered her guard, the stakes would go up, way up, and she had to decide if the risk was worth the consequences she might have to suffer later. *Might. Later.* Those were the key words that sealed her decision.

"All right, then," she acquiesced. "We'll take it as it

comes, see what happens. But, Noble, I've gotta tell you, I'm really scared about this."

"I know you are, Lori. I know." His soothing voice held a silken edge of mystique that stole her breath and tantalized her imagination. "How very brave you are," he continued while turning her toward the table. His chest to her spine, his lips to her nape, he leaned in and led her hands to the cloth-covered bread. "So very brave to confront your fears and come with me to a place only the two of us can go."

"Where . . . where are we going?"

"On a journey. A journey of the senses. Close your eyes," he gently commanded.

Lori could feel her heart hammer, her belly clutch in anticipation of the sensual unknown, as she shut her eyes. "Why?" she asked.

"Quite simply, I want you to look within as we explore a world of our making—a very intimate realm where trust is earned and forged. Come with me, Lori," he murmured, guiding her unsteady hands to uncover the bread, then lightly stroke its warm, crusty surface.

It felt good, so good and reassuring. Instinctively, she sought the source of its heat, and sank her fingertips deep into the loaf. The steam seeped beneath and around her nails, and she indulged in the sensory delight.

"Do you like the feel of my bread?"

"I do. It's like holding hearth and home in my hands."

"And such is the way I feel when I hold you." His arms came around her waist, and in his embrace she felt a wondrous, lifting thrill. The strength of his chest pressed to her back, his arousal firm against her, quickening her own desire. And the bread's giving texture, wrapped around her fingers, felt wonderful, like a moist cloth to a fever.

There was a fever inside her, rising high and fast in her blood. Noble. Noble was the fever. He was in her system and all she could do was pray he didn't break her.

But for now she was safe, safe in his whispered promise: "No need to fear the next leg of our journey, I'm here and holding fast to you, love." There was a sweet restraint in his touch as he glided his palms from her knees to her thighs, too slowly raising her skirt and bathing her neck with leisurely kisses. By the time he hiked the skirt over her hips and stroked her buttocks until she moaned soft and long, her need for more, so much more, was dire.

"My hose," she panted. "Noble, please, take them down."

"Far be it from me to refuse you a second time," he assured her with a low, seductive chuckle. His thumbs hooked into the elastic, and she could hardly bear the suspense as the blunt edge of his nails skated down her legs. They were trembling, unsteady, when he reached her knees. There, he stopped. Before she could demand that he finish, he placed a demand of his own.

His hand covered one of hers, leading it away from the security she clutched. He placed her palm over the knife's hilt.

"You know what I want you to do," he whispered,

his breath moist, hot on her nape. At her halting nod, he let go. "Courage, Lori. You've come so far, don't falter now. Freedom, release, they're within your grasp. *Trust me.*"

Disbelieving of what she was doing even as she did it, Lori drew the knife down and put its blade to the panty hose stretched taut between her knees. Her hand shook as she sliced awkwardly at the elastic band.

"Help me?" she whispered.

"I would be honored, my love," came his hoarse reply.

Lori felt the rip as surely as the rending of her frail defenses. Noble slid the spliced panty hose down, taking them off until nylon and shoes and defenses lay at her feet.

She kicked all three aside and was rewarded with his approving groan, a lingering kiss to each bare-bottomed cheek. Rising, he stroked her belly with a sweeping caress. And then she endured a delicious agony, the feel of him fretting her most private hair, the teasing graze of his fingertip to the peak of her gender's pulse.

"Make love to me," she pleaded, then demanded, "Make love to me, Noble. Now. *Now.*"

"All in good time," he said with a maddening calm while he drove her nearly insane with the slide of his palms between her legs. She eagerly opened them and he bent his knees to the backs of hers, fit himself to her everywhere except for where she was desperate to be joined together, tight as a fist gloved in wet velvet.

She thrust back, urged him on with a frantic push of her hips. "For the love of God, what are you waiting for?" she all but shrieked. He stilled her with a firm clamp.

"Patience, Lori," he soothed her. "One should never rush what's meant to be savored." His hand wound into her hair and she felt the tug prickle her scalp and tingle her womb. He pressed her down until her cheek rested on the linen tablecloth and the earthy aroma of yeast invaded her senses.

She smelled the bread made by his hands, smelled the clean scent of his skin riding hers, and weaving around and through them both was the smell of musk, pulsing on waves of a dizzying, sexual heat.

Where was this place Noble had taken them? she vaguely wondered. The answer came swiftly. This place, this intoxicating, mind-bending place, was where the unknown became the known and more than bodies were bared. It was a place of intimacy as she had never perceived it before, racing on a current of the deepest reaches of desire, buried in the far corners of her mind. Hidden, until Noble had taken her where she'd never dreamed to go . . .

His realm. He ruled here with ease and dark grace. His passion controlled while he unleashed her own, so completely and profoundly that she didn't hesitate to obey him. "The butter, Lori. Hand me the butter," he commanded.

She passed him the semifirm stick. He skated tiny figure eights over her nerve ends until she pounded the table and begged for him to stop, only to plead for the butter's return when he did.

She heard the butter thud onto the table, felt his grip on her arms just before he abruptly turned her to face him. Her eyes flew open and she struggled to focus on his looming face, his breath coming harsh and fast while her own was nowhere to be found.

"What—what are you doing?" she gasped out.

"The better question is, what are you allowing me to do?"

"I . . . I don't know."

"But of course you do. Think, Lori. *Think.*"

She struggled for coherence. "Whatever you want," she managed to say. "I'm letting you do whatever you want."

"Exactly. But why? Tell me why," he demanded.

"Be-because . . ." Why *had* she let him do what he'd done? And with her eager assistance, no less. It was crazy, made no sense. But then came a flash of insight and it made all the sense in the world. She had the answer and she knew it was the answer he wanted. Swallowing hard, she whispered, "Because I trust you."

"Very good." The approving nod of his head made her realize she had just been taught a lesson by a master logician whose methods had left an indelible impression. In her head, in her heart. And it sure as heck didn't end there.

"Okay, Noble, you made your point," she conceded, past ready to pick up where they'd left off.

"Then you realize what I need from you, what you need from me, can't possibly be relegated to a bed?"

"Yes!" She threw up her hands in exasperation and

her grinding frustration rose to a dangerous level when he softly chuckled.

"In that case . . ." Noble kissed her soundly then swept her into his arms and took the stairs, two at a time. "Off to bed with us."

THIRTEEN

The scent of vanilla snaked through the air, rising from a dozen flickering candles. They lent his quarters, the bedroom of his request, a soft illumination, a perfect complement to the vision Noble beheld. He thought Lori ravishing as she undressed, quaintly shy, unquestionably eager, ravishing in her proud nakedness as she slipped into an exotic gossamer gown.

She was soft and lovely, such a stark contrast to the hard jolt seizing his groin. But even harder was the fisting in his gut now that the moment of his own body's display was at hand. Perhaps the candles would make the sight less jarring, he told himself, knowing full well it wouldn't.

"Do you like the gown?" she asked, the transparent silk floating around her like a whisper as she came to him, laid her palms on his chest.

"It's divine, love," he assured her, winning a pretty blush as he traced the lacy bodice. "Almost as divine as you." His heart quickened from her nearness, but then Lori began releasing the buttons of his shirt and it beat faster, thudded with dread as his shirt fell to the floor.

She pressed her cheek against his heart.

"I love your chest, Noble. But not just because it's beautiful to look at. I feel your strength there. And it makes me feel strong, too—almost as if you're sharing some mysterious power with me."

"You are strong, Lori. Stronger than almost anyone I've ever known. Perhaps what you feel is your strength meeting mine. Meet it now so I might borrow some of yours?" Steeling himself, he explained, "I have something to show you which I've taken care to keep from your sight. It is not pretty to look at, I must warn you."

"What is it, Noble?" She searched his gaze, concern brimming in her eyes.

Noble took a steadying breath, then forced himself to turn.

"My God," she gasped. He could feel the fine shake of her fingertips as she traced the shape of the letter J branded between his shoulder blades. "Who did this to you?"

"A few bloody bastards who gave me a permanent reminder that I was not welcome in Juneau. They were the same men who killed my parents and stole our land. When I returned to demand a rightful legal justice, this was the justice I got."

"But didn't the sheriff do something? Arrest them or—"

"No, Lori." He laughed darkly. "The lawman stood by and watched as they did it."

"How could he do such a thing? I—I mean, it was his job to protect you, not let some horrible men commit such a brutal crime."

"Those horrible men fairly owned the city. While I spent my years in England, they filled the bank with my family's gold and claimed a wealth of power. It was a minor thing, really, to have a lawman in their pockets."

"I've never heard of anything so . . . so obscene." She laid her palm over the brand and he silently gave thanks she hadn't recoiled, had spared him her pity. "If something like this happened today, those men would be put behind bars and that sorry excuse for a sheriff would lose his badge and probably do some time himself." Voice seething, she said, "I can't even imagine living in a society as twisted as that."

Noble was certain what she said was true. And because she couldn't imagine it, neither could he expect her to imagine the thrilling satisfaction he had taken in committing murder. The twisted society had twisted him, this he could not deny. Perhaps it was why he felt no remorse or shame for his own monstrous deeds, only a gut-deep fear of Lori's rejection once he confessed them. Oh, but how he did loathe his lie of omission. It was between them, separating them. But it was Lori's modern sense of justice keeping him silent.

"There is much about your society which is twisted as well," he pointed out. "You lost your husband to a robber with a gun. A tragic crime. Yet, from what I have read in your papers, there is no end to the brutalities against innocent people. Is it any wonder some take the law into their own hands when your current legal system fails them?"

"Two wrongs don't make a right, Noble. As much as I'd like to kill the bastard who shot Mick, as many times as I've dreamed of doing it, I couldn't and still live with myself."

Carefully, he tested the bounds between them. "But if you had killed him in retaliation for your loss, I would form no ill judgment of you. Indeed, Lori, I would understand and feel no less for you than I presently do."

He endured her hesitation. "I wish I could say the same, Noble, but that's your time talking, not mine," she replied. She kissed his back and he felt branded all over again, marked by the sweetness of her lips. "Let's just be thankful we survived," she whispered. "There's a special closeness between us, and strange as it is, I think we owe part of it to having gone through a lot of hell to touch a piece of heaven together."

Shutting away the past, Noble faced the woman he could lose with a single, shattering revelation.

"Yes," he agreed. "To look at you, to touch you, is to know that I have been blessed. It's as if I fell asleep in hell and woke up in the arms of an angel. That's what I thought when I first saw you, the light glowing like a halo around your golden hair."

She laughed softly. "And your second thought was that I was a harlot." Her eyes holding his, she unfastened his belt. "Maybe I was in a past lifetime. All I know is you sure have a way of bringing out the harlot in me."

Lord, but he did love her. Noble gripped Lori to

him, embraced both angel and seductress. With her smiles and tart tongue and bungling attempts at seduction, she had aroused his body beyond measure, laid open his most hidden emotions, which he had learned to hide ever so well.

"Be my harlot," he said into her ear. Be my wife, he beseeched her in silence.

"What do you want?" she asked, sliding down the zipper, pulling down his pants, taking them off, kneeling at his feet.

"I wish for a most intimate kiss, my saucy wench. But first, what shall it cost me?"

"More than a pinch of gold." Looking up at him with a simmering, liquid gaze, she named her price. "One good kiss deserves another. However, I do expect a little accumulated interest when you pay up."

The sound of her sultry laughter filled his ears while he felt his most vulnerable flesh embraced by her mouth. *Vulnerable.* Never in his life had he felt so vulnerable. Not to anyone or anything. Not even when his face had been shoved to the ground, his shirt ripped open by a knife, and a branding iron put to his back while scream after scream ripped from his throat. Despite it all, he had not been abased, his pride had not been conquered.

And yet here Lori was, conquering his body, his very soul, until he begged her to cease and desist. With no pride at all, he demanded an equal justice.

He paid the price she had named—with an exorbitant amount of interest.

"Enough," she screamed. "Enough!" She dragged him up by his hair and covered his face with kisses.

The need, the absolute need to take her, immediately and with a savage passion, was blinding, and how close he came to taking her on the floor. But then he remembered her wish for protection, the small box she had laid on the nightstand. He carried her to the bed and hastily shook open the box of sheaths. Enough to last them a few days, he supposed. Nonetheless, he'd go to the store after he visited the law library.

"Will you put it on me?" She slid the sheath on him and, once done, kissed the shield. The sight was enormously arousing, but he cared not a whit for the barrier between him and her lips.

"I like doing this," she said with a throaty sigh. "If it's all the same to you, I'll do it for as long as we're together."

"That will be a very long time, if the gods are as gracious as they've been thus far."

Lori pulled him on top of her. "Be gracious, Noble. Be where I want you now. All of you inside me. And whatever you do, please don't be polite about it."

Despite her demand, he was respectful of her body's resistance, testimony to her celibate years. He descended, ever so slowly giving her his flesh and blood now as he kissed her with a possessive hunger.

She whimpered his name, and he fought the urge to plunge. For if he did, it would be over too soon, and this night he would give her release upon release, seal their intimate bond, and mark her as his.

The condom helped rein in the demand of his instincts to thrust until they were bathed in sweat and collapsed on lust-drenched sheets. The vision proved too tempting and Noble tried to block it from his mind. This was what he'd been waiting his whole life for, what he felt with Lori now. And what a gift it was, to have been inside many a woman's body and yet, with this slow slide into Lori's, to feel like a virgin again. A rare and wondrous thing, he savored his painful restraint and knew what he had now was what his parents had had.

Good, life had been so good. And then . . . as always he tried to shut out the massacre, the other painful, horrible memories. In reflex Noble pulled up and aggressively surged down, damning himself at Lori's sharp cry. But then she cried out again, arched her hips, and sank her nails into his back, and he heard her sob in ecstasy, not pain.

She bit into his shoulder and it snapped the leash of his control.

He had no control. None whatsoever over the flood of his emotions or the ravaging pump of his hips. From a distance he heard himself call to Lori, entreat her to take his poison, his love, the fury of his passion.

She took them all. It was ease he sought and ease she gave as they writhed amid tangled sheets and sweat-slick limbs.

Suddenly his coming was upon him. With a last, primal lunge, Noble stared down at Lori, who opened her eyes to him. Her gaze was wild and feverish, as was his own, and she chanted his name like a prayer while, in silence, he pulsed within her intimate embrace and touched the threshold of . . .

Home.

He was home as never before, and yet, as they rocked together in the aftermath, Lori crying while he sipped at her tears, Noble was shaken.

"Are you all right?" he asked with concern, not sure if he was all right himself.

"I—I feel like I'm in a thousand pieces, and if I let go of you, I'll fall apart."

"Yes," he whispered. "Yes, I feel that way exactly. I've . . . Lori, please forgive me for behaving as I did. Not even with a harlot have I ever been so rough, so stripped of self-control. And you, you are a lady deserving of gentleness, your body honored with care."

The gaze she turned on him was soft as her fingertips traced the scratches her nails had scored on his back.

"My body has never been more honored, Noble. I can only hope you feel the same way. Never, *never* have I clawed my way down a man's back." She kissed his shoulder, the place which slightly stung and bore the imprint of her teeth. "I can't believe I did this." She kissed another mark on his chest. "Or this."

"But you did and I loved it. And now, knowing only I have ever driven you to do such a thing, I love it all the more." They shared a small, pulsing silence. "It would seem, Lori," he said slowly, "that we have discovered something remarkable with each other that we didn't expect. How lucky we are to be graced with such a startling surprise. And how wrong we would be to disgrace it with our apologies. Apologies imply shame and there should be no shame between us for what we have been blessed to share."

Lori nodded. And then she said, hopefully, "Is it really true that you treated me worse—or make that, better—than you ever did one of your harlots or courtesans?"

"Absolutely," he answered without pause. "Though I gained a reputation as a skilled lover, I apparently presented a bit of a challenge. Or so I was told on a few occasions. It seems I was perceived as rather remote and much too courteous."

"Why? After all, you were paying them to have it however you wanted and I'm sure they would have been glad to oblige."

"Quite true. But I wanted it with the safety of distance. There's the difference, love. I want no distance from you." He felt her hand wrap around his base, felt himself responding with remarkable speed.

"Mmmm. I never was one to back down from a challenge. Let's see if I can make you even less courteous than you've already been."

"Lori," he warned, "much as our first time means to me, I fear to subject you to a second until I fully collect myself." And he did. She had stripped away the defenses that protected him, and what was in him was so dark, so deep, that once it was fully unearthed . . .

God help them both.

"Do me a favor, Noble?"

"I could deny you nothing." A vow, it was true.

"Don't collect yourself. I want you rough and I want you sweet. Every way you can be, I want *you*."

FOURTEEN

"Want another strawberry, Ryan?" Lori tapped one into a heap of sugar and popped it into her mouth. Maybe if she kept herself chewing, she'd quit trying to fill in the awkward silences.

"No thanks. By the way, quite a layout here. You really outdid yourself, Lori."

"Noble put it all together," she said too effusively. "Hey, if you think this is great, just wait till you take a bite of his bread." She felt Noble squeeze her knee, a secret gesture to acknowledge the secret seduction they'd shared. But he kept his gaze trained on Ryan, she noticed uneasily, just as Ryan kept his on Noble.

"Lori, love," Noble said, emphasizing the endearment, "would you mind fetching the cognac? I'd like to indulge in a finer spirit than tea over strawberries and lox. Perhaps you and your, ah, friend here, will join me."

"Fine by me," Ryan agreed, unsmiling.

"Cognac for three coming right up." Lori was almost relieved to leave the room, though she worried about leaving Ryan and Noble alone.

"Okay, she's gone." Ryan shoved aside his untasted tea.

"But not for long, so let's have at it, shall we?"

"Lori's got it bad for you, and that's got me worried."

"As well it should." Noble felt a grudging respect for the man who had minced no words with his rival. "She's obviously very fond of you, which disturbs me as well. Clearly, both of us care deeply for the woman."

"You bet I care. Did she tell you how her husband died?"

"She did. An abysmal, nightmarish thing."

"A nightmare is right. I was with her when Mick was brought in. I was there for the funeral, too, and I've been there for her ever since. I love Lori. I've loved her for years. And I'll be damned before I ever watch her go through hell again."

"Your devotion is admirable. However, you have no further need to 'be there for her.' "

"Because you're here, right?"

"But of course."

Ryan glanced toward the door. "You're sleeping with her, aren't you?" he said in an accusing whisper. "Gotta hand it to you, man, you didn't waste any time. She's been wobbling into work with a glow on her face a blind man couldn't miss in the dark."

Noble came over the table and seized Ryan by his shirt. "No gentleman would ever divulge such matters.

And no gentleman would presume to ask such a thing. You, sir, have overstepped your bounds. Do so again and I'll call you out. Lori is my woman now and I will not relinquish her to you or anyone else. Just as I will not tolerate even a hint of disrespect shown toward her, not by word or deed. If you should ever touch her in an unseemly manner, I will break the hand you put on her. Heed my warning and heed it well."

He released Ryan with a jerk and prepared for an attack. With surprise, Noble watched the other man settle back in his chair, the hint of a smile twitching his lips. "So, you'll break my hand if I make a pass at her, huh?"

"Are you so foolish as to take my vow lightly? Lori does care for you, though not the way you apparently care for her. For Lori's sake, please spare me the need to send you to the hospital for reasons other than work."

Ryan reached toward his hip and Noble automatically reached for his. Just as he cursed his missing gun, Ryan laid a lighter and a small pack of cigars on the table.

"Lori said if I wanted to impress you, I should come bearing gifts. I waited for you to impress me first." He took out two cigars and extended one. "I'm impressed."

After a small hesitation, Noble took it. "I do not understand. Explain, please."

"It's like this, Noble. I won't give you any cause to break my bones if you don't give me any to break your neck. If you hurt Lori, I will. As long as you're good to her, we'll get along just fine."

"You mean . . . you do not want her for yourself?"

"Hell, no! That'd be like marrying my sister." With a hearty burst of laughter, Ryan offered his hand.

Noble gripped it, then flicked the lighter and put the flame to the tip of Ryan's cigar before lighting his own.

Feeling quite pleased with the outcome of their confrontation, Noble blew a smoke ring. Ryan coughed and sputtered then managed to wheeze out, "So, want to join me and the boys for a few rounds of poker? We've got a game lined up for a week from tonight."

Noble flicked his ashes. Hmmm. Perhaps there was more than one way to provide for Lori, even if his mother lode of gold dust was dry. Or if by some miracle he couldn't pass the state bar. Already he had absorbed a volume of ground-breaking cases at the law library. Fortunately, the study of law came as easily to him now as it had when he'd graduated, top honors, at Cambridge. The difference was, he now took a bus, not a carriage, as soon as Lori left for work, and returned in ample time to prepare dinner—in the microwave.

"Poker," he drawled, studying his cigar. "Actually, I'd very much like to play poker with you and 'the boys.' Not that I'm very good at it, but I'd enjoy a respite from watching cartoons and Geraldo—though there's little difference between the two that I can perceive."

"Oh jeez," Ryan groaned. "Something tells me to bring along only as much as I can afford to lose." He glanced warily at the door. "If you want to okay this with Lori before we count you in, no problem. I don't want to rock the love boat, if you know what I mean."

Actually, Noble didn't. Ask permission of a woman, even one dearly loved, before placing a wager? Unthinkable.

"Of course you can count me in," Noble blithely replied.

"It still wouldn't be a bad idea to—" He stopped short as Lori returned, holding a regal-looking decanter filled with amber liquid.

"I couldn't find the cognac," she said with a little catch to her voice. "Did you put it somewhere, Noble?"

He had. On the dresser in his room just prior to the tea, anticipating a confrontation with Ryan and stealing time for it as Lori went in search. What he had not anticipated was her retrieving another bottle. "Crown Royal!" Ryan exclaimed. "Tell the truth, Lori. You bought it because it's my most inaffordable vice. Who says men get paid more than women? Hell, you make more than me."

Crown Royal. Lori's anniversary present to Mick. Ryan did not know this, given the way he dumped the leftover contents from three teacups into Lori's sink. "Gimme that," he demanded with a grin, and then broke the bottle's seal.

Before Ryan could pour, Noble gripped his hand and returned the bottle to Lori. Bending close, he whispered to her, "Save it if you wish. I'll gladly fetch the cognac and bring Ryan along with me so you might have a few moments alone."

She wrapped an arm around his neck, pressing her anniversary present between them. "Thanks for understanding, Noble," she whispered into his ear, "but I can't keep time in a bottle. I'll do the honors."

She filled their teacups to the brim and lifted hers. "A toast," she proposed. "To new beginnings."

"Here, here," Ryan said, looking from one to the other.

"But let us not stop there." Noble spoke directly to Lori. "Toast with me to happy endings."

Three teacups touched and then Ryan moved away, seeming to realize this was a moment for two, not three.

Noble linked his arm through Lori's. Their gazes locked as the two of them lingered over a thoughtful sip that was more a prayer.

"You're going *where*?"

"As I said, to play poker with Ryan and his friends," Noble said casually, pulling on a second boot. Standing in his room—where they now slept instead of hers—he clicked his heels smartly. "No need to drive me, Ryan should be here shortly. By the way, thank you again for the driving lesson today. Oh, and have I mentioned I've committed to memory the rule book you gave me on highway protocol and regulations?"

"Twice." Great, she thought, just great! Another few lessons and Noble could drive himself to a poker game —minus a license, since he didn't have a birth certificate. "Know when you'll be home?" she asked, trying to sound indifferent.

"When the game is over."

When the game is over, she silently mimicked as he

breezed by her, patting her rear as he passed. He lifted a large-framed print from the wall, removed an envelope pushpinned behind it, and withdrew a stack of bills. Twenties. At least ten of them.

"This is where I keep my money should you have need of it, or should I meet with an accident—"

"Don't even say that," she snapped, feeling the whiplash of the past.

He came to her, his gaze full of the understanding she had come to need so desperately, despite her attempts not to. With each passing day she needed him more, and it terrified her. Even if she didn't lose Noble to another woman, she could lose him to a car accident tonight, tomorrow, next year.

"Lori," he said firmly, gently, "you can't live in the shadow of fear, else it will dwarf all that is bright and good. What might be, is just that. What *is*, is all that's certain. And for a certainty, I absolutely adore you and can't wait to awaken you upon my return. Now give me a kiss for luck. The sooner I collect my winnings, the sooner I'll collect your affections in bed."

Fat chance, she wanted to tell him. Instead, she bit her tongue and said, "What makes you so sure you'll win?"

"I'll win. *After* I deliberately lose a few rounds." His smile was smug as he leaned down. "My kiss?"

She gave him a peck on the cheek, then turned away before she said something bitchy.

Noble's hand shot out and he whirled her around. "With a kiss like that, I'll be lucky to break even."

"What's this? You're superstitious?"

"No. But I am perplexed as to your behavior. Could it be that you actually begrudge me an evening away from you when you spend most of your days away from me?"

"That's different." She hated this conversation. The best thing she could do would be to give him a big kiss and send him off with a smile. But no, here she was sounding like a shrew. "I go to work to make a living and you're going out with a bunch of beer-swigging guys to play poker."

"The more they swig, the better, so they might forget to guard their expressions. Bloody hell, Lori, much as I relish a good game of poker, I'd far rather be with you. However, as you've pointed out, you go to work to make a living. I, on the other hand, am currently denied the same privilege. Do not resent me for seeking what earnings I can by what means are available to me."

You've got a gun, so go work for the mob. Ashamed that she'd even thought such a thing, Lori said, "Sorry, Noble. I hope you win big tonight."

"But not just for myself. Please understand, I do this for us. It grieves me greatly when I hear you say, 'I wish I could stay home with you instead of going to work.' You say it each morning, and each morning I long for the day when I shan't hear those words again. That day will come, Lori, I vow to you it will. Be patient. Indulge me tonight. And remember, I keep my vows."

She was considering how to explain that she really liked her job—and even if they got past all their hurdles, got married, and he won the Publishers Clearing House

Sweepstakes, she'd still want to work—when a horn sounded outside.

Ryan. No big surprise he'd honked instead of knocked. The chicken.

"You'd better get going," Lori said, knuckling his strong, stubbled chin. "Good luck, Noble. Come home with lots more money than you left with, and a few shirts thrown in."

He smiled. Seductively. "Actually, I am a bit superstitious when it comes to cards. Will you grant me luck with a kiss to match what winnings you wish me?"

She laid one on him.

The horn honked again.

At the door Noble patted his pockets. "I'll win," he told her. "And return with a few shirts added to my wardrobe."

Lori didn't doubt it. After all, he'd played each and every card right with her.

He took her heart out the door with him and she knew there was no getting it back.

Lori glared at the clock. Ten o'clock on the P.M. With a disgusted snort, she threw down the cross-stitch sampler her mother had given her two Christmases ago. For therapy.

Therapy was *not* stabbing her finger with a needle while she waited for a man to rack up his winnings and come home. Therapy was shopping. Therapy was eating a box of chocolates and watching old Cary Grant movies. Therapy was doodling on cover models' faces.

But most especially, therapy was unloading on another woman who could provide sympathy as well as shrewd advice.

Besides, she and Jenn needed to have that heart-to-heart she'd been too busy with Noble to have. Jenn, a sharp cookie but not exactly a rocket scientist, had swallowed the excuse that Noble was breathing but wasn't up to company since his brain had yet to completely thaw out.

More than thawed, he continued to blow her mind. Lori didn't doubt at all that even now he was blowing a hole through Warren's and Jacob's pockets. Jennifer deserved the next introduction. Maybe she'd put their meeting off because the next step would be for Noble to meet the rest of her friends, gal pals included. First driving, then poker, the inevitable socializing at her hangouts wasn't far behind.

"Hey, Jenn, wanna hit the Kick and Kaboodle?"

"Say, gal, where've you been? No, don't tell me, you've been having a mad, passionate affair with the hunka-hunka burning ice while I've been painting my nails."

"Yep. If you want the scoop, meet me at the club in an hour."

"Make that fifteen minutes. I'm already out the door."

"Last call!"

Ignoring the call, just as they had a dozen dance

offers, Lori and Jennifer continued to huddle over the small table.

"Okay, Lori, from what you've told me, this guy is to die for."

"If he dies, I'm dead, Jenn. He is so under my skin, it scares the hell out of me. After Mick, I just barely survived. But now I'm living again. Really living, like never before. Only, if I lose Noble, I'll—"

"Survive. You'll survive, Lori. Only the strong survive and you're one of the strongest people I know."

"That's what Noble says, but I don't feel strong. When he touches me, I can't think. When we're apart, he's all I can think about. And when we're together, I'm so happy I could cry. Sometimes I do, but mostly I laugh. He makes me laugh. He makes me think. He makes me ache. He makes bread."

"Know what, Lori? If I were you, I'd be scared too."

"If you're trying to make me feel better, you're not."

Jennifer gripped Lori's hand. "Look, toots, the best advice I can give you is to hang tough and hang on to that man." Jennifer got up. "Go home, Lori. There ain't nothing around here to compete with this Noble of yours."

Lori took a look around. "Know what? You're right."

"Damn right I'm right. Now be a good girl and go home."

Lori gave her a high five. "Better yet, I'll go home and be a *baad* girl."

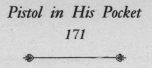

She was awake, tossing and turning in the too empty bed, when she heard Noble's tread on the stairs.

Unlike most men coming home at four in the morning, he didn't try to sneak in. He gave her a soft kiss while she pretended sleep; she listened to the domestic sound of him tossing off his boots along with the rest of his clothes.

Climbing in beside her, he palmed a breast and whispered, "Are you asleep?"

Even if she had been, she wouldn't be now. The feel of his chest to her spine, his lifting of her leg, and the partial arousal he wedged between her thighs before closing them back, was more than even a zombie could ignore.

"I won several hundred dollars tonight," he confided in a murmur. "It's not much, but it is a beginning. There's so much, Lori, so very much I want to give to you."

"Then give me," she demanded, nuzzling as close as she could get. "Give me you."

FIFTEEN

"Are you kidding me? Noble, you can't be serious."

"But I am," he said, sloughing off lather and whiskers into the bathroom sink. So much had changed in the six weeks he'd lived with Lori that he found himself holding stubbornly to old habits, disdaining such things as electric razors and plying his whiskers with a straight razor and hard soap. He took another sweep, then paused when he saw her glaring at him in the mirror. To her reflection, he repeated, "I am serious, Lori. Though I appreciate your endeavors to gain me a new identity, I have no intention of assuming it."

"Why not?" she demanded. "You had two before."

His wince earned him a nick. Controlling his expression, Noble said reasonably, "My past is just that and I make no apologies or excuses for who I am now—Noble Zhivago, son of Boris and Diana Zhivago. As for the birth certificate you got a copy of, it belongs to Barry Jones, who, were he living, would surely not want me to take his name and birthdate any more than I wish to steal them."

"You're not stealing anything, you're just . . . borrowing some identification."

Noble narrowed his gaze at her reflection. "Believe me, I know the difference between stealing and borrowing. To take a man's name and rob him of his birth date, *that* is stealing."

"Okay, call it what you want. But the man is dead and has no use for them anymore. You do. Without that birth certificate you can't take a driving test and get the license you're so hot to have. And without a driver's license you can't write checks or—"

"Enough." He threw the razor into the sink and faced her squarely. "I am who I am, and that is that. I am not an actor pretending to rehearse his role for a movie. Neither am I Barry Jones, for he is dead. But Noble Zhivago? Why, he's quite alive. I am a proud man, Lori, one who is equally proud of his identity and heritage."

"Fine! You should be proud of it. Just be careful to keep it to yourself. I've told you, how many times, what could happen if the wrong people found out the truth about you. They'd be all over you and—"

"Just let them try." He sneered. "I have no fear of these people, though they should fear me should they attempt to steal my freedom."

"Okay. Okay, so you're not afraid of them. But I am. Do you hear me, Noble? *I am*. If they tried to take you away from me—" Her voice caught. He reached for her, but Lori pulled away. "Don't you understand how much you mean to me? Damn you, Noble. Damn you for coming into my life and making me need you and want you so much that it hurts."

"Might I take that as a profession of love?" Let it be, he silently beseeched her. If she would only tell him that she loved him, fiercely, beyond reason, then he would take the ultimate risk. He loathed this thing between them, his criminal past. He loathed it a thousand times more than this petty bickering over his real identity, which he would have to expose once his secret studies at the law library were done. He loathed it far more than his grinding frustration to search for his gold, something he could not do until he revealed all to her. Which he would do now if she would simply say it.

"Say you love me, Lori." His eyes spoke a demand, a plea.

"I—I . . ." She shook her head, averted her gaze. "I'm sorry, Noble, but I'm not ready to say it yet."

"Why not?" Gripping her chin, he forced her to look at him. "You sleep with me, you give your body freely to me, share your joys and sorrows. If that is not love, what is it?"

"It's a lot, that's what. What we have is really special and I need it so much I'm scared it's too good to last. I could love you, Noble, in a heartbeat I could. But once I let it happen, I'll want it all. I'll want forever. You've made incredible strides in a very short time and—and I'm still afraid you might outgrow me."

He smacked a fist into his palm and fought the urge to shake some sense into her. "For such a fearless, intelligent woman, I am amazed by your aptitude for daftness and sheer cowardice. You refuse to give up your blinders and see what's staring you in the face. And why? Because you choose to be a prisoner to fear. Fear of my progression. Fear of your emotions, fear of mine. Fear of my lack of fear. Bloody hell, Lori, you're so consumed with fear, it's a wonder there's room left inside you for anything else! No, you couldn't possibly love me yet, not when you're so damn afraid to put love ahead of what's eating you alive."

He turned his back to her.

"Tell me," he demanded, "should another person ever chance to see my mark, how would you have me explain it?"

"You'd never show that to anyone," she hedged. "Not unless it was another woman you trusted enough to show it to."

"And not unless I was rushed to your workplace, bleeding and broken from some accident. Alas, two more of your fears I neglected to mention. Other women and sudden death."

"It's not that I don't trust you, it's other women I don't trust. Hell, we can't even go into a grocery store without me having to watch my step so I don't slip on the drool."

Though he wished to empathize with her, as he so easily did, Noble felt none of that now. All he felt was a deep disappointment as Lori once again took three steps forward, two steps back. His patience was wearing thin.

"Have I not vowed to you, despite your foolish and tiresome belief otherwise, that no other woman but you will do in my life or in my bed? Unfortunately, I cannot vouch for the fickleness of time in meeting one's Maker. Should I meet mine tomorrow, how would *you* explain my mark to those curious people, save Ryan, who would see it on my corpse?" When she hesitated, he snarled, "Dammit, Lori, answer me. The truth."

"I . . . I'd tell them it was a tattoo. A botched-up tattoo job. Or something else just as ludicrous, like— like you'd had a wild past and been a member of a gang and it was part of the initiation rites."

"And you actually believe such excuses would be more lauditory of my past than the true horrors of it?"

"No." Her palm to his brand was a fire in itself, branding him more surely than his tormentors had. "But if I told them the truth, if by some miracle they believed me, they'd probably take you apart with a scalpel. Rummage around your organs to see what they looked like. Expose your brain to see if brains were different a hundred years ago than they are now, and gnash their teeth because they lost the chance to squeeze you dry for information while you were alive."

"But what should I care if they wished to dissect me? After all, the dead feel no physical pain."

"Maybe the dead don't, but the living do. It would tear me up if they tore you apart and treated you like a specimen who wasn't entitled to a shred of dignity."

Noble tapped his lips. And then he put his on hers. Parting a whisper's distance, he said solemnly, "My dignity belongs to me and only to me. No one can take it away, not even with a knife. But you, Lori, as always you cut too deep. Far deeper than any surgeon's blade ever could. You cut me to the quick and lay open my heart with your tender mercies for this untender man."

"Untender?" She shook her head. "You're one of the most tender men I've ever known. Even if I could, I wouldn't change a thing about you. *Except* for that infuriating stubborn streak of yours that won't listen to reason."

"Alas, you're right. Stubborn I am." Noble pinched the defiant jut of her chin. "And so are you." He chuckled.

Lori didn't laugh with him. He was taking this too lightly and she wasn't ready to give up.

"Don't let your pride get in the way of good sense. Please, Noble. Use the birth certificate."

"As Shakespeare once said, 'To be or not to be, that is the question.' Let it be, love. For now, just let it be."

"Only you"—she sighed—"only you would make a closing statement quoting the Bard and the Beatles."

"They say much of the same in their disparate ways. Their words are framed by insight and emotion rather than the passage of time. So it is with you and me." He leaned down and she felt the warm fan of his breath as he repeated, "So it is with you and me."

His coaxing whisper, the taste of shared air, was more intimate than a kiss. How easily he made her desire him, with a word, a look. And how easily he could persuade her, even when his reasoning made no sense at all. Not for the first time Lori winced inside at the terrible unfairness of his awesome talents going to waste.

Only it didn't have to be that way. If only he was willing to listen, she could explain her plan, the reason she had selected Barry Jones as the perfect identity to steal. Or rather, borrow. Permanently.

Accepting a temporary defeat, she said with certainty, "You were one hell of a lawyer, weren't you, Noble?"

"Actually . . . yes. I was quite ruthless in the courtroom, and much in demand. Rather like I am in bed, only I kept my clothes on and limited my passion to the stating of cases, the thrill of win after win." He softly bit her bottom lip. "I'll win you as well, Lori."

There was little doubt in her mind that he would. Noble slapped down the defenses she put up when the fears pressed in with the ease of a swatter to a fly. Even now he was making her melt with the slide of his thigh between her knees, the span of his hands gripping her jean-clad hips while he pressed her against the bathroom wall.

"Come along now," he murmured. "Come for a ride with me. Hold on tight and I'll guide the reins."

Hold tight she did, her nails biting into his shoulders and eliciting a low, lusty growl at the harder, higher rub of his thigh until she stood on tiptoe.

What had begun as a trot ended on a gallop. A short but breathtaking ride. With a smile of supreme satisfaction, Noble caught her up in his arms.

"I rest my case," he said with a satisfied laugh. "I'll win you yet, Lori. Even if I have to ride you into the dust to do it, I will win your heart for my own."

From there he carried her to his room and tossed her onto the bed. Maybe the fall knocked some sense into her, or maybe it was just that she had stopped hyperventilating and the oxygen kicked into her brain. Whatever, she was hit with the pinpoint realization that Noble had been right. He had his act together and knew his own mind. She was the one standing in their way, not he.

"Let's go to the Kick and Kaboodle tomorrow night," Lori said quickly, before she changed her mind.

His pants drawn down to his thighs, he paused. "Very well. But why do you sound so . . . so resigned to visiting what was once your favorite dance hall? The one you've taken to shunning despite our lovely Jennifer's open invitation to join her there," he said pointedly. "Not that I'm overly inclined to go myself, but why do you suddenly wish to go?"

"Because I've decided to tackle my fears instead of holding us back. One at a time—Rome wasn't conquered in a day. First things first, I'm going to introduce you to my competition and try not to throw a pitcher of beer at them or anyone else who asks you to dance."

"A woman ask a man to dance? How odd."

"Get used to the idea. They'll be asking, Noble." She got up, switched on the clock radio to a soft-rock station. "I'm first in line." Quickly, she took off her jeans, her top, and held out her hand.

"Dance with me? Dance with me naked in broad daylight. And once we're done, how about a dance between the sheets?"

Their discarded clothes piled in a heap, they danced their first dance.

Fred Astaire and Ginger Rogers they weren't, Lori decided. She stepped on his toes. He clenched her waist too tightly and grumbled, "Quit trying to lead. I'll do the leading. Follow me."

As it was with most everything else in their relationship, after their share of missteps, they managed to be in sync. By the third song, she thought him a smooth and wonderful dancer—though a little overbearing in his leading and overly purposeful in his footwork, as if he had considered each turn and anticipated her reaction before she did.

By the time he dipped her and she clung to his waist for support, Lori was dizzy. Dizzy with delight. Dizzy with the fear she was determined to face the next night. He'd sweep each and every woman there off her feet. And he wouldn't even have to dance with them to do it.

"Let go," Noble whispered. "Let go of me and reach for the sky. No questions, just do as I ask."

She let go, only to gasp as he released her. A moment before her back hit the floor, his palms scooped under her to cushion the blow. And then he laid himself atop her, his chest to her breasts, her toes to his shins.

"What was *that* for?" she demanded.

"It was for you and it was for me. For us. A lesson, if you will, in letting go and trusting me to be there even when you fear I won't."

His full weight upon her, Lori rocked her hips against his. And as she did she knew a fierce want to claim those parts of Noble that remained in the past. She wanted all of him, not just what she had now.

An idea that had been brewing surfaced. "Tomorrow's my off day. Let's go for a drive. To your land. We can pack a lunch, you can show me around, and we'll spend the afternoon there."

Why was he so silent? she wondered. Was he afraid a subdivision had taken the place of his parents' house? Was he afraid to confront his worst memory by going to where it had taken place? Was this why he hadn't asked her to take him there before?

"Hey, it's okay if you don't want to go—"

"We'll go." Without a smile, a kiss, he rolled off her and sat. Though he was only a few inches away, something about his posture was remote as he reached for the bedside table. Rather than the box of condoms she had expected, he took a cigar and studied it for a long time before lighting up.

Lori noticed that his hand shook slightly. "What's the matter?" she asked, scooting next to him.

"Nothing," he said shortly. He stared at the smoke rings he set afloat and she felt a terrible sense of desertion.

"That's not true. You never smoke in the bedroom and—why won't you look at me?"

His hesitation wasn't like him at all and she felt he wanted to be alone. It hurt her, this invisible distance he was putting between them.

"Let me be where you are now," she quietly demanded. "Tell me what's bothering you and let me be there for you like you are for me."

He cut his gaze to hers and she was stunned by what

she saw. Lori cupped his cheek. "You're afraid of something. What is it, Noble?" she whispered.

After a thoughtful pause, he turned his lips into her palm. "What do I fear? I fear the lack of your love," he said, pulling her tight against him. "Just that. Nothing else."

SIXTEEN

The house no longer stood. All that was left was a pile of crumbling bricks, what had once been a chimney. A few charred and splintered beams were scattered about; the house had burned.

With the buzz of a sawmill filling his ears, competing with the roar of the past, Noble felt his heart contract in a tight, painful fist. He had not truly wanted to venture here, knowing he might be greeted with a disaster such as this.

From the looks of it, the place had met its sad end decades ago, surely before Lori was born. Somehow the fire had been contained to the house and surrounding area, where lush green grass now grew. The nearby forest, where he had played under Attu's watchful eye, had been spared by fire. The once magnificent red cedars and white spruces were now a legion of stumps, gone the way of the sawmill and likely framing thousands of other homes.

He closed his hand around a brick and squeezed what was left of his beloved home. It was late spring, a lovely, gentle time of year. But the chill wind that blew inside him was like winter.

Had Attu been there, he would have walked away, allowing them to tend their silent grief separately. But not Lori, for here she was laying her hand over his own.

"Do you want to be alone?" she asked gently.

Did he? In his past life, he had always withdrawn into himself, nursed his wounds and his black anger in solitude, wanting it that way because those poisons were his and his alone.

"Stay," he said, his voice tight and scratchy, rough. "I wish for you to stay with me, Lori." Her touch eased him. It assuaged his sense of loss, the toxic emotions churning through him.

For a long time they simply stood there together, staring out at the butchered forest, listening to the distant drone of the sawmill while he absorbed the comfort she gave him in their shared silence.

He let the past wash over him and then ebb away. Noble released the brick and threaded his fingers through hers.

"There is nothing for me here," he said with a heavy sigh. He led her toward the car parked on the makeshift road, rutted from lumber trucks that had hauled his childhood playground away. With more force, he said again, "There is nothing for me here. Except you." He lifted her hand for a grateful kiss. "And that is more than I had when last I saw the place. In truth, it's easier to see the house gone than it was when I stole through the woods and spied upon the murdering thief and his wife who resided there as if it were their own."

"Then you came here after you returned from England."

"Once. Just once. That was quite enough." He decided to make her privy to a portion of his plan—but not the means by which he acted upon it. "I vowed that when I next came here, it would be to take possession of what was rightfully mine. All ten thousand acres, along with the home. Since the bastard couldn't live forever" —*and since I would see to it once I had seized back my family's fortune from the bank the bastard owned*—"I determined to purchase the holdings from his widow. She was much younger and had a frivolous nature. I thought it safe to assume she would sell if the price was right."

"Whew, you're talking a lot of loot. Where would you ever come up with that kind of cash?"

He chuckled softly yet watched her carefully as he said with a light tone, "I considered robbing a bank."

Lori flinched. "Sorry, but I can't see the humor in that. Call it one of those sensitive nerves I have."

Her reaction was no surprise, but it troubled him, increased his dread for the inevitable moment when he put his love on the line and hers to the ultimate test.

Quickly rerouting their conversation, he said, "Forgive my poor attempt at trivializing what was indeed a serious situation. You're right, it was a lot of money. However, the gold mine was bled dry and the logging business wasn't much of a business yet. And so the land was worth only a pittance of what it must be worth now, even with so much of the forest stripped. Yet it was, and still remains, worth more to me than a king's ransom."

She squeezed his hand, letting him know that she understood, felt the weight of his hope, his loss. This was good, he decided, a step in the right direction. "I had a dream of living on my land, taking a wife and raising children where I had spent the happiest years of my youth," he confessed.

"That's a beautiful dream, Noble. I wish it had come true."

"Even if it had, it would have been lacking." He turned, caught her shoulders. "After all, I wouldn't have had you."

Her reply was a soft, catching sound, more than a sigh, less than the profession he longed to hear.

"So, here we are, back to your chariot of steel," Noble said, sounding more chipper, and he hoped less eager than he felt. "Would you care to see the mine where my father struck gold?" He knew she wouldn't venture far inside due to her aversion to closed spaces, but as with many of Lori's confessions that had come back to him, he deemed it strategic to keep this to himself. Too much of the lawyer was in him to reveal all that he knew when such knowledge kept him a step ahead of the judge and jury.

"Check out the mine? Hey, that'd be great! At least, I'd like to see the outside of it." Lori, too, sounded as if she were trying hard to lighten the somber atmosphere of dashed dreams and tremulous hope. "Want to drive?"

"Absolutely." He handed her into the passenger's

side and bent down, their mouths hovering, their eyes meeting in anticipation of a kiss slow in coming.

The moment was meant to be savored and this kiss held a significance beyond any they had shared before. Just as he knew it would be, the first, light touch of their lips sealed his past and their yearning to claim a future together. It was a lingering, lushly passionate kiss that ached with emotion and hummed with the swelling tide of dreams.

Lifting his mouth, he told her with his gaze how truly, how very deeply he loved her.

"I know you do, Noble," she whispered aloud to his silent message. She held his face in her hands and glowed. "Be patient with me? Time's on your side, but it's slipping fast from mine."

Returning her smile, he nodded his acceptance. "As any good lawyer knows, timing is everything. So is winning."

"The Long and Winding Road" was playing on the radio as he pressed the clutch and slipped the transmission into overdrive. His own inner gears were in overdrive as well. The sheer thrill of mastering the powerful machine was eclipsed by a full-throttle rush of anxiety and anticipation.

"Slow down!" Lori yelled over the music while she clung to the door and stomped her foot hard on the floor.

Noble forced himself to let up on the accelerator, and they bumped over the rough dirt road at what felt like a crawl. "Either slow it down or I'm taking the wheel," Lori commanded, and he dropped to a snail's pace of thirty on the speedometer.

"That's better," she gasped out, patting her heart. "Good Lord, what's the big hurry anyway? It's not like you've got a claim and someone's trying to jump it."

He couldn't take his eyes from the jutting formation that finally, *finally*, came into view. "Sorry, Lori," he said with false calm. "What with no stop signs or speed limits to heed, and no worry of getting caught without a license by one of your friends, I suppose I got carried away."

"I guess," she said with a huff. "Just don't get carried away again or I'm taking back the keys."

"Duly noted," he muttered, his attention focused on the mine, which was so close now he could feel it. Lord, but he could even smell the dank air, hear the echo of his footfall bounce against the jagged tunnel walls as he trod the maze to where he had hidden his gold. *His*, dammit. He had not robbed; he'd merely taken back what was his.

Somehow, he would have to make Lori understand that. Surely an easier task than making her understand his taking of lives. Even if time were on his side, his patience was already at its limit. He so wished to be done with it, to tell her right now and hurry inside the mine, which beckoned. At long last there, Noble almost forgot to put the car in park and kill the engine before he leaped out the door.

He approached the mine, forcing himself not to

race. And smacked a fist against the barrier of wood and the "Warning Condemned" sign that blocked the entrance.

It took all the willpower he had and then some not to rip the sign off and charge through the wood.

"What's the matter, Noble?" Lori came up behind him and he quickly replaced his hideous grimace with an expression that he hoped passed for mere disappointment.

"I so wanted to explore at least a little of the mine. It was, after all, where my father and I spent many hours talking as he allowed me to mine a bit of gold myself."

"Sounds like a special memory."

"Yes." Relieved that she had taken his explanation at face value, Noble went on with a small, tender smile. "The Aleuts who worked for Father weren't mistreated as so many had been by other Russians. They would mine around us and offer me an occasional pointer, tell me a native joke I didn't understand but laughed at anyway. And I could always expect someone to sneak me a sweet treat just before I left, along with a warning that there would be no more if I told my mother, close as it was to dinner. . . ."

He trailed off, remembering it all and wishing it back.

But even more fiercely he wished for some way to open the cave and make straight for his hiding place while he prayed that the gold was still there.

"What an incredible life you've had." Lori hugged his waist, looked up at him with wonder sparkling in her eyes. Wonder and compassion and perhaps even a little envy. "If you can, just be thankful for a wealth of memories. Nobody can take those away, Noble. They're yours to keep."

What she said was true. Nonetheless, he knew those memories wouldn't be enough. New memories and dreams shared with Lori, his status as a lawyer to be reckoned with and a new home built where his old had burned, that would be enough. Yes, a grand home built for them both and their children with the sacks of gold it would take to claim such a dream, that would be enough.

"Still feel like going dancing tonight?" she asked, sounding unsure if she felt like going herself.

"Seeing that you're tackling one of your fears, then by all means, let's be on our way so we can get on with this matter of the heart."

She laughed dryly. "And I thought you were going to be patient. You don't sound too patient to me."

"Perhaps I should increase your own impatience so it might match my own." He shrugged out of his light jacket, laid it at the cave's sealed entry. "Here. Here is where I'll have you. Immediately and without protest. A new memory, Lori, to transcend those of the past."

Lori did not protest. An urgency gripped her as she shed her clothes in the great wide open and laid on the jacket, still warm from his body.

She opened her arms. He came into them.

Noble entered her without further ado and she was more than ready for him. She took him easily, her womb yearning for his blunt and solid touch. If she could have, she would have taken him all the way to her heart. Her heart, where he touched her as insistently as he did her body.

She called to him, demanded he meet her need with his own. He came then, spilled his seed on her stomach, her name spilling again and again from his lips. Her wrenching cry of "Noble, Noble" was soulful and loud before his lips crushed and silenced her own.

The music was noisy and so were the people about him, shouting over the music to make themselves heard.

Scanning the crowd at the Kick and Kaboodle, Noble decided that he and Lori were the only ones who said more in silence than the rowdies managed in their strident laughter and abrasive yells.

It was not so different from the other dance halls he'd been in; tame, actually, in comparison. Women did not lift their skirts and seduce men into their rooms so they might part with their gold in exchange for the parting of legs.

Even so, he did not like this place. And judging from her false smile as she yelled something back to their friend Jennifer, Lori had ceased liking the dance hall herself.

While he studied her and sipped silently at his beer, a woman approached him. A comely woman, were her hair not so artificially blond, her clothes so tight, and her makeup so generously applied.

She asked him to dance. He looked to Lori for help,

silently pleading with her to tell the other woman that she'd already been promised this dance. But, no. She smiled. Grimly. "Go ahead, Noble. Dance with the lady."

Dance with her he did. But a lady she was not, giving him coy smiles or licking her lips while she "accidentally" brushed her breasts to his chest. The woman was worse than a harlot. She offered him her body for free when he hadn't the least interest in taking it.

Nevertheless he thanked her for the dance and sighed his relief once it was over. He did this again and again, barely able to sit down before another woman approached. Most of them were far more pleasant and genuine than the first, but only good manners induced him to accept their invitations.

He did not want to dance with these women. The woman he wanted to be with was Lori. Lori, who pretended not to notice his vacant seat at the table while she yelled back and forth with Jennifer and darted her eyes to the dance floor. He intercepted each chance glance with a befuddled, accusing gaze, which she turned from as if unable to bear the sight of him with another woman, though she had all but pushed him into their undesired company.

"Last dance!" was called out. As he made his way to the table, thirsty for more than a sip of beer to wet his mouth, he felt yet another tap on his shoulder.

Noble turned. The woman was absolutely beautiful by any standards of time or man. She looked quite sure of his answer as she crooked a finger.

"Thank you. But, no. The last dance goes to my lady."

He left the disgruntled woman and approached Lori who was smiling for the first time all night.

Extending his hand, he asked, insisted, "Dance with me."

She came out of her seat faster than he could pull her from it. And then . . . then, oh, how they danced.

Without a care in the world for what others thought of them, they flowed together as a river wide and just as deep. Never mind that it was a line dance, everyone else dancing alone. Together they danced in the middle, claimed their own realm, and didn't bother to apologize to anyone blocking their way as they forged a singular, whirling path.

It was only after the music ceased to play, after he bent her back and ravaged her mouth with a demanding kiss he'd longed for all night, that silence surrounded them. And then, the sound of a clap, followed by another and another until the rafters echoed with applause and shrill whistles came at them from every direction.

He shifted his mouth to her ear so she would hear him over the roar. "I don't want to be here, Lori. I want to be with you, only with you."

"My bedroom or yours?"

Noble hesitated before answering her. The wedding picture had posed too much of a threat to make love to her where he most wanted to.

"Yours," he said firmly.

"Then what are we waiting for? Let's split before

the second encore." They received a second encore anyway as he swept her into his arms and made for the exit.

Lori had let Mick and her past go. Starting tonight, Noble determined to do the same.

SEVENTEEN

"No-ble. Oh honey, I'm ho-ome," Lori singsonged, her step happy and light as she sailed into the kitchen. She was two hours early, the first of several anniversary presents.

For three months they had lived together in glorious, passionate bliss—if she didn't count their occasional arguments. Which always ended in more glorious, passionate bliss.

She took out the lobster tails she'd bought, along with a bottle of *un*cheap champagne and a pound of real butter. Smiling mischievously, she left a stick out on the counter. Appetizer enough, Lori decided. Besides, she was cooking dinner for a change, so they just might have butter for dessert, too.

Hopefully they'd have enough left for the lobster.

At that last thought, she giggled on her way to the stairs, her new nightie and a black silk robe for Noble in hand. Also in the bag was a framed candid of them kissing that Ryan had taken. She'd suggest they put it in place of her wedding picture, which belonged in a photo album, not beside a shared bed.

But first, she'd give Noble the best present of all. Three words she couldn't hold back any longer.

Did she love Noble? Not much. Only madly, completely, without question or fear. He hadn't pressed her to say it since that day on his parents' land. Neither had he said the words himself, stubborn, marvelous man that he was, waiting for her. But he told her in a thousand different ways.

Waking her with a rose tickling her nose, then sweeping her from head to toe with the petals. Chiding her when she said she didn't have time for breakfast and insisting she eat on the way. Tending a small cut with a kiss to make it better. Chasing her through the house then tickling her until she screamed for mercy, only for Noble to show no mercy at all, a suddenly serious man who was as purposeful in his dark passion as he was in all else.

He read extensively, lightning fast, and delighted in challenging her with spirited debates. Even though she rarely won, he left no doubt of his respect for her opinion. Noble, her Noble, was a rare and wonderful man, whose skill at poker was rivaled only by his ability to make the best bread ever.

Better enjoy it while she could. He was too ambitious to play househusband much longer.

There. Her biggest fear confronted. Marriage. Marriage to a man who was nothing like Mick and everything she could ever want. Noble, who would be a wise but stern, patient but playful father. She wanted children. *His* children. She wanted his name. But . . . Noble didn't have a name in the eyes of the very law he should be practicing. Such a waste. Such a damn waste. If only he wouldn't cut her off every time she brought up the birth certificate . . .

Her smile fading, Lori felt a familiar frustration. It wasn't right that he refused to establish a new identity. Without it, he couldn't get any kind of a license, marriage included. But surely *that* would be incentive enough to change his mind. She held the trump card and this was one hand she was sure of winning.

Approaching the bedroom, Lori paused, mentally arranging her words that probably wouldn't come out right anyway.

First, she would tell him he'd convinced her his love and loyalty were true. Then she'd tell him that she had come to realize life held no guarantees, and even if he died tomorrow, the pain would be worth it because she wouldn't trade a single minute they shared for a lifetime of never having known him.

And then . . . then she'd tell him she loved him.

If he didn't propose, she would. Once they got that settled, she would convince him to use the birth certificate so they could get married and get on with their lives. So what if they shared a borrowed last name? Both of them would know it was Zhivago and nothing else mattered.

He wouldn't like it. But if Noble wanted to marry her badly enough, surely he could swallow his pride. They could fly to Vegas and he could meet her parents, who had retired there. He could formally ask her father for her hand, as she was sure he would do—and then, then . . .

Squaring her shoulders, Lori took a deep breath and marched into the bedroom, prepared as she'd ever be to take charge of fate.

His name was on her lips, but he wasn't there. She searched the house, calling to him.

Where was he? With a sigh of disappointment, she decided he must be out and about somewhere within walking distance.

Lori decided to use her time alone in a soothing bath. With bubbles, lots of them. Then she'd put on her new nightie. Who cared if it was the middle of the day? Noble sure wouldn't. He was the one who had taught her the value of sheer feminine whimsy.

Lord, she thought, for having such a serious nature, he sure had a way of bringing out the naughty in her.

And she was feeling naughty when she heard him rummaging around the kitchen. Eager as she was to race down the stairs and tell him her insights and professions and even propose if he didn't beat her to it, Lori stayed put on his bed where they'd first made love. Draped as alluringly as possible she greeted him with a sultry, "Hi, lover. Happy anniversary."

He stopped abruptly at the open door. And looked from her to a legal pad in his hands.

"Lori?" he said with an untypical note of uncertainty. "What are you doing here?"

"Waiting. For you." When he didn't move, she beckoned him to the bed. Again, he looked from her to the pad. Something that resembled guilt, not the delight and purely male heat she had expected, shadowed his face. "Something tells me that wherever you've been has a lot to do with the fact you're not ripping off your clothes and jumping my bones."

His conflicted gaze meeting hers, Noble silently handed her the thick sheaf of pages filled with his script.

He wasn't taking notes on Shakespeare. An uneasy feeling twisted her stomach as she flipped through enough legalese jottings to make a Supreme Court judge's head spin. Her own pounded an echo of *oh no, oh no, no, no, no.*

"You were at the state law library, weren't you?"

"I was. It's where I go once you've gone to work. It's where I leave an hour before you arrive home. It is where I've been tutoring myself with a vengeance so I might take the state bar. Another year, perhaps less, and I'll be ready."

"But to take the bar you have to have proof that you graduated from law school."

He looked at her then, directly and without apology. "I have graduated from law school, Lori. Top of the class, Cambridge, 1887. Furthermore, I have proven myself as a force to be reckoned with in a courtroom. As I shall prove myself again once I finish with my studies and pass the bar."

"I'm sure you could do it with your eyes closed, Noble. But that doesn't change the fact that you don't have a diploma—"

"I do. Not the original, but the photocopy I received last week will suffice."

"That photocopy has your name on it."

"As well it should. I earned my law degree, Lori. And now I have the proof that I did. All I need to do is convince the necessary authorities it is indeed mine, which I will, and then I'll take the bar. Since one's reputation isn't earned overnight, you'll likely have to work awhile longer, but once I'm established, you need never work again."

"But I like my job," she said frantically. "Never mind that, forget my job for now—"

"I *never* forget it. Have you any idea how it galls me to see you off to work when more than anything I want to go to my own? Have you any inkling of how I long to kiss you and our children, leave with the knowledge that my family is well provided for and safe? Safe in a grand house on my land—*our land*—that will never see blood shed upon it again. This is my dream, Lori, a dream so real it's in every breath I take."

Her own breath was a pant of panic. The one fear she had convinced herself she wouldn't have to face was coming at her head-on and Lori floundered as wave upon wave assaulted her.

Fighting for calm, she knew this was one battle she had to win. "It—it's a wonderful dream, but the price is too high. You want too much, Noble. The only way we can have even a piece of your dream is if you're willing to compromise."

"And just what do you propose?" He sneered. "That I continue to tend the house, minus my studies, while you continue to support us both, my own paltry means of support limited to the occasional poker game?"

She knew, had known all along, that Noble couldn't live like that and neither could she. He'd start to resent her while she tried to make everything all right, and she'd end up resenting him when she couldn't. In the end what was so good between them now would turn sour.

"You haven't wanted to talk about it, so I never told you why I picked Barry Jones from all the obituaries I could find. Out of state—he was from Nebraska."

"Of course. After all, it wouldn't do for me to pretend to be someone I'm not when others here could recognize me for the imposter I would be."

There was a cutting edge to his voice that made her wince. But she couldn't back down.

"Listen to me, just hear me out, okay? The picture they ran of him slightly resembled you. He was in his midthirties, no wife or kids. He was also a lawyer, Noble. *A lawyer.* The obituary listed his credentials, where he'd graduated. It shouldn't be much harder to get a copy of his transcripts and diploma than it was to get the birth certificate. People lose things like that all the time, right?"

At Noble's stony silence, she rushed on.

"You couldn't practice in his city—even the same state would be risky. But you could take another bar and work in almost any state you wanted to. We'd have to move, at least out of Juneau, since people who know me might ask questions, but I don't care. All I care about is making a life together. A good life, Noble. I'm begging you, *please*, swallow your pride and bend your principles on this. If you could just do that, we could get married, have a family—"

"Shall I take this as a profession of love?"

The light of hope in his eyes made her hope too. Now he would listen, see reason. She wrapped her arms around him. "Yes. *Yes*. I do love you, Noble," she assured him, passionately. "It's something I can't fight anymore. We're right together, so damn right. You won, counselor. You won for us both. We can have it all. *Let us have it*."

He kissed her deeply. Then pulled back and shook his head. "How I have longed to hear those words from you. But, Lori, we can't have it all if we're living a lie. And that's what it would be. The truth has a way of emerging sooner or later, and it would. Perhaps out of the mouths of babes; children tend to speak without guarding their words. Would you have me hide my heritage from any offspring we might be blessed to have? Would you have me give them and you a name that is not mine to give while I deny my own?"

He placed his left hand over hers. "Come and grow old with me. The best, Lori, is yet to be."

God knew it had to get better than this. She was in misery, what she'd been sure would be one of the best days of her life, a shambles.

Lori searched for the strength to pick up the pieces and emerge with a fellow survivor: Noble Zhivago, barrister-at-law, who had won yet another case.

"Okay, Noble. We'll do it your way. Finish your

studies, convince who you have to convince that you are who you are, in order to take the bar, and we'll deal with the scientists and the media. Together." She tossed the pad aside and got up, pacing the floor. "Am I crazy or just in love?" she debated, her eyes to heaven. "I'm so in love with you that I'm crazy with it. It's gonna be awful, Noble. Really, really awful. But before it gets bad, let's enjoy it while we can."

She held out her arms. Noble took an eager step forward, then stopped. In the small distance he searched her eyes and whatever he found there caused him to swallow hard. So hard Lori could see the contraction of his throat.

"What's the problem, Noble? Something's wrong."

"Indeed, Lori, something is wrong. Very wrong. A lie stands between us. It is my lie and one I've loathed. But I kept it so that I wouldn't lose you. If your love is everything you say it is—and I pray God it's so—then you will love me still, despite the ugliness of the truth."

"Whatever it is, it can't be half as bad as you make it sound." His anguished gaze told her it was. A terrible sensation came over Lori, made her scalp tingle, the hair on her nape stand on end. "Hey, it's not like you killed someone or something," she said, forcing a nervous laugh.

With a low curse, Noble lifted the mattress and withdrew a folded piece of paper.

"Before I show you a dark bit of my past, I'll have you know it also holds a promise for the future. The mine I took you to—you see, it possibly contains more than memories. If so, we can reclaim the land which rightfully belongs to me and build where my house once stood. Whether or not the means to that dream is still there, I'll take the bar. The love of law runs too deep in my veins not to."

"Okay, okay," she said anxiously. "We've got the bar thing settled, okay? But what's this business about some dark past?"

Noble fingered the paper and hesitated, causing her apprehension to mount. When he replied, his words were measured and careful. Too careful.

"Please, Lori, keep in mind that wealthy people enjoy a good degree of protection which is denied those with lesser means. We could claim our dream and some immunity from the curious as well if we were shielded by the power which comes with money. To be exact, a fortune in gold. *My* gold. I seized it from those who took it first. Whether or not it's still in the mine where I hid it is the only question remaining."

"The *only* question remaining?" she repeated as a buzzing noise filled her ears. She wanted to cover them, run from the room and pretend she hadn't heard any of this. Instead, she heard the questions tumble out, wanting to stop them and not wanting to hear his answers. "Where did you get that gold, Noble? What did you do to get it?"

He gave her the folded paper. Hands trembling, she slowly opened the aged page, and a nightmare leaped from the past and into the present.

She stared at it, the roughly drawn picture that was

unmistakably Noble, the words that her mind refused to register:

WANTED

LUKE LASSITER

FOR ARMED ROBBERY AND MURDER

$5000 REWARD

DEAD OR ALIVE

Lori wanted to throw it down, throw her head back and laugh, accuse him of a really sick joke, and tell him that she loved him anyway, that both of them knew he was Noble Zhivago, barrister, not some Luke character who robbed banks and killed people.

"It's strange, but I get the feeling you're two different people in one."

"But of course I am. I assumed Attu told you."

"I only knew you needed help and you're lucky—"

"Lucky Luke." A chuckle. "So, Attu failed to mention my real name? Allow me to introduce myself . . ."

Their first meeting replayed itself without mercy, flashed before her the way people's lives supposedly did just before they died. Lori heard the sound of sloshing water, felt the consoling sweep of his embrace while he tasted her tears, and she claimed a personal victory so transcending she could smell its sweetness even now.

She stared in disbelief at the truth that made everything they had shared a lie.

Numb, she felt so numb. It was the way she'd felt when she had touched Mick's cold, still hand in the coffin, unable to believe she was really there and he was gone.

It had seemed so horribly unreal. Shock had a way of getting people by until they could handle the trauma. A part of her knew she was in shock now, but this was one trauma she couldn't imagine ever being able to get over. She was trapped in a nightmare and she was desperate to wake up from it.

"I love you, Lori."

It was a man's voice filled with passion and conviction. But it wasn't Mick's voice saying that he loved her. Neither was it Noble's. It was the voice of a stranger she heard, one belonging to a robber and a murderer. The same breed of lowlife who'd crawled out from under some slimy rock to demand money with a gun before turning it on her good, decent husband. Drowning in his own blood, killed with a bullet in his heart, another in his face.

"I love . . . you. Lori . . . sweetheart . . . sorry, so . . . sorry."

Mick had begged her to forgive him for dying. And now she begged him to forgive her for living. For coming back to life again, thrilling to the touch of a man who had pulled a trigger of his own.

"I love you, Lori."

There were the words again, suffused with truth and longing and every gut-deep emotion a human could feel. But she didn't want them. She didn't want them any more than she could stand to feel his hands gripping her arms.

"Don't touch me," she snapped, jerking away from

his fierce grip. She thrust the wanted poster at him, as if it were contaminated. Unable to bear even looking at him, she gave him her back.

"Lori, please—"

"Don't touch me." She shrank from his beseeching whisper, slapped off the palm he gently laid on her shoulder. "Don't ever touch me again. You're tainted."

EIGHTEEN

Don't ever touch me again. You're tainted.

The words rolled over and over, uncountable times, lashing him more cruelly than his grandfather's cane, seared into him with a pain more severe than a scalding iron.

He had braced himself for the worst, but this was immeasurably worse than he'd allowed himself to imagine.

His hands balled into fists and it was all Noble could do not to shake her until every memory fell from her head and onto the floor so he might stomp upon each one until Lori's mind, her heart, was left blank and unscarred, able to accept the man who loved her now.

"All that is truly tainted is your past and mine," he said to her rigid back, desperate to make her understand. "For the love of God, Lori, don't throw our future away for the sake of what can't be undone and is better forgotten."

She whirled on him, eyes snapping cold fire. "You're right, it can't be undone. For the rest of my life I'll never be able to wash away the guilt for letting you put your bloodstained hands on me. Get your things, Noble. Just get them and get out."

For a while he could only stare at her, disbelieving that her love could turn so quickly into this vicious rebuke, which bordered on hatred.

Get his things? He'd get them, all right. He got his gun from beneath the mattress and held it out to her.

"Go ahead, Lori. Take it. Fill it with the bullets you hid in your lingerie drawer. I'll wait while you do."

Her chin slightly trembled and then she lifted it. "That's your brand of justice, not mine. Keep the pistol. It's not worth it."

His hurt and desperation blended with a familiar rage, one he clung to as fiercely as he would make her cling to him before he took his leave.

With a hurtling, savage throw he heard the shatter of a mirror. It echoed the shattering of his hope, the shards his dreams.

The ensuing silence crackled with livid emotion. Then Noble tore off his shirt, throwing it toward the broken glass.

Lori backed away, hands raised to ward him off.

Noble seized her, laughed darkly as she slapped at him, beat at his chest. "Let *go* of me!"

"All in good time. But first, you'll hear what I have endured. And once I am done, I'll hear you beg for my touch."

"*Never.* Touch me, and so help me, I—"

Noble crushed her mouth with his. He assaulted her lips with the force of his rage, the unbearable pain she had inflicted as if she had bitten into his very soul. Suddenly her teeth sank into his bottom lip. Though it stung sharply, he reveled in covering his mouth over hers, painting her lips with his blood. He made her taste what she had drawn. The very life of him, of his ancestors, even of those children they might have had.

But he would make her want him, *him*, just as he was, dammit, and he'd take a bittersweet victory with him when he left.

Hauling her into his arms, Noble took a savage pleasure in her struggles, and then the feel of her body pinned beneath his on the bed, where he would have his say before exacting his vengeance. Great as his urge was to rip aside the flimsy bodice, he gently cupped a barely covered breast and squeezed it as if it were her heart he held in his hand.

At her whimper, which she surely detested as much as he prized it, he assured her, "I would never rape you, Lori. Rape is a violent, evil thing. Not only for the victim but for those who love them, who would gladly die to keep such an atrocity from happening to their loved ones. This I know because I have witnessed it—"

"I don't want to hear this." Her voice was as frantic as the shake of her head. He stilled both with a hard palm to her mouth.

"This is how I was rendered silent while I watched from my mother's large, deep wardrobe. She had pushed me in, with Attu. She gave me a last kiss, commanded Attu to hold me fast and keep me silent. I struggled to break free and opened the door a crack before Attu subdued me. I saw my mother being thrown to the floor, her clothes ripped with a knife. And all around me I could smell her, the perfume she wore that clung to the folds of her dresses, silky, soft, hugging me as she never would again."

Noble drew a harsh, ragged breath and forced himself to go on, forced Lori to go where he had been, where he was each day of his life.

"She was brutally raped by three men while she cried for mercy, cried to my father, who was held with a gun to his head. Attu commanded me not to look. I commanded myself not to look. But I couldn't tear my eyes from this unspeakable thing being done to my mother, my father. I couldn't stop hearing her prayers, my father's pleas to kill him and spare his wife. I'll never stop hearing them. No more than I will the sound of two bullets. One to my mother's head. And then my father's."

Noble took his hand away from Lori's mouth.

"I don't want to hear any more," she choked out. "Enough, Noble. *Enough.*"

"Pray God hears you better than He did my mother, because you'll get no pardon from me." Despite his warning, Lori no longer struggled against him. Not even when he slid up the tiny skirt of her nightgown and put his hand between her thighs.

It was retribution he was after, seeking it and claiming it with a single, caressing finger between her intimate folds.

"For a truth, I am tainted," he whispered while

sweeping his lips over hers. "For a truth, blood is on my hands. The very hands which I lay on you now. Would you have me remove them?"

"After—after what those men did to your parents, and then, later, to—to you, it drove you over the edge, that's all. You weren't responsible for what you did."

How easy it would be to play upon the welling sympathy in her watery gaze. How easy it would be to agree to Lori's flimsy excuses for what he had done. She needed those excuses to accept him, but even more he needed her to accept him as the man he really was.

Noble laughed once, grimly, refuting her desperate attempt to still love him.

"Oh, but I was, Lori. I was fully responsible for stealing back the gold which was stolen from my family. Just as I claim full responsibility for shedding blood so vile that I delighted in the taking of it. I have no more remorse for what I have done than they had for their own acts. My only regret is that the last living bastard, the one who first raped my mother and planted a bullet in my father's head, met his end by some means other than my own hand."

She closed her eyes to him, moaned softly. It was a mournful sound, like the whistle of a chill wind rattling brittle, leafless branches. A lonely sound filled with yearning for a beloved, lost companion.

Noble knew that companion was he.

"Do you wish me to leave?"

"No," she whispered.

"Then do you wish me to stay?"

She opened her eyes and he saw a terrible sadness,

confusion, the flicker of a reluctant arousal. Lori shook her head, nodded, then covered her face with her hands.

"I don't know. I don't know anything anymore, Noble. I don't want you to leave, I don't want you to stay. I love who you are now, but I can't stand who you were. I don't know who you really are. I have no idea who I am. All I know is that I still want you and I wish to God that I didn't."

"Because my touch disgusts you?" He swept at his lip and put a single, bloodstained finger inside her. Her body grasped it, then her hips arched to deepen his delving.

"What disgusts me is *me*," she sobbed out. "Me, needing what you're doing when I know that very finger pulled the trigger of a gun. It makes me as sick with myself as I am with you. If—if only you regretted—"

"But I don't," he said hotly. "On my mother's grave, I swear to you that I regret none of it. I'll have no more lies between us, Lori. Therefore, should your need transcend your disgust, then open your eyes and look at the truth."

"But I don't want to look."

"Either you look or I'll be gone."

She looked then, from his hand that dipped inside the skimpy bodice and palmed her breast, to his gathered fingers entering her body again and again with an inexorable slowness.

He felt her internal walls grip him, then reluctantly give him up. It was almost as wonderfully satisfying as her little whimpers, the sight of her gaze turning from disgust to desire.

He withdrew his hand. She grabbed it back.

"No. Don't leave. Don't leave me like this."

"Then how shall I leave you? And leave you I shall, Lori. I can no more live with your guilt and uncertainty than you can live with my past crimes. Any future we might have is up to you since I can't change what I have done. All that can change is your inability to accept me for who I am. Would you accept the whole of me now? Or simply that part of me which feeds your need?"

She hesitated, then parted her thighs. "You're right, Noble. You have to leave. Maybe for an hour, a day, a lifetime—however long it takes me to come to terms with this horrible thing. But make love to me now. Make love to me and make it all go away. And then . . . then, after you're gone, I'll think."

He respected her honesty. And much as he detested this piercing farewell, Noble was grateful for the truthfulness of it. The truth, the whole of it, was finally out and any touch they shared from here on was honest, not shadowed by deceit.

He sent a prayer to heaven that she might love him still, more fully than before. And perhaps heaven was listening, for he saw in Lori's eyes that she didn't despise him anymore. He rendered her naked with haste, little gentleness to be had from his hands, which stroked her again and again, so mercilessly, she could barely draw air.

Her frantic jerks at his pants were an echo of the rawness of their emotions, their sad, desperate need. Within seconds he was poised to fill her with that part of himself she begged for. *Beg for all of me, my name, my blood joined with yours in our progeny*, he silently pleaded, but Noble commanded himself not to enter the comfort of her body.

"Please, Noble. *Please.* Be inside me."

"But only to visit, not to stay." He ravaged her mouth with his until, by force of sheer will, of pride, he made himself utter the ultimate truth.

"Whatever is between us is only what remains between you and your past, not mine. I have laid myself bare. You trampled upon my remains and yet here I am demanding that you take all that is brutal and ugly along with the best of me. If you would have me inside you now, have all of me, man that I am."

"Make love to me," she begged.

"Men like me don't make love. They're driven by demons and the darkness inside them. The darkness, it's hideous, so hideous and vile. I am that darkness, Lori. But when I'm inside you, you cleanse me. Dear God, how I want that from you, to take it with me when I go. But I'll leave now if you don't take all of me at least this once."

"All right," she sobbed. "All right! I want all of you."

He gave her all of himself. Body and soul. She writhed and moaned and cried all at once while he pumped into her, ridding himself of the demons that tarnished his past, their present. He spilled their future onto the sheets between her thighs.

Lori was still racked with her own release when he got up.

He dared not hold her, console her in the aftermath. Should he do that, he would never be able to leave.

While she lay sobbing on the bed, her eyes closed to him, Noble gathered those things that had seen him from a glacial crevasse and into her house. Hers, not theirs. There were too many ghosts here; if they ever survived this destruction, they would have to start anew, pick up where their separate pasts ended, and forge a future together that was strengthened by understanding and unconditional love.

Buckskin pants on, Noble donned a simple white shirt. He shoved the empty pistol into the holster riding his hips. Not that the impotent weapon would do him any good when facing an enemy.

He confronted his greatest enemy now, Lori's rejection and uncertainty filling his chest as he stuffed his feet into his boots. The click of his heels on the floor and Lori's jagged sobs were the only sounds to be heard as he went to the door.

He swallowed against a burning tightness and said as evenly as he was able, "Tainted though my touch might be, my heart is pure. It has killed purely. It has loved purely. Please know that I do love you, Lori. I would have you for a friend beyond measure, the mother of my children, a mate who transcends the title of wife. But this is as I would have you, not as you are willing to be or wish to have me in equal measure. I'll wait for you, even if it's in another lifetime that we meet to settle the score. Until your own demons are laid to rest, fare thee well, my lady."

He left then, but paused in the hallway, hoping

against hope she would race after him, call him back. But Noble did not even hear a whisper of his name while his heart thudded dully in his chest, echoed from ear to ear.

His eyes were dry, so dry they stung from the moisture dammed behind them as he walked with resignation down the stairs and whispered to no one but himself, "Fare thee well."

NINETEEN

How long she lay there, Lori couldn't say. Time had no meaning while she stroked the sheets that carried his scent and she breathed him in as if she were drowning, gasping for a sustaining wisp of air. And all the while she tried to hate Noble for putting her through hell and back, making her live his nightmarish memories.

For killing her softly with his tainted touch.

But is it really tainted, Lori? Of course it is, she answered herself. He's robbed and done murder. *Then why aren't you taking your damn bath, washing away the last traces of his filthy hands on you?* Because . . . because— all right I don't *feel* dirty. But I should. I should feel like I've wallowed in mud instead of feel loved inside and out.

But what about your heart that you gave to him, no holds barred, then took back in the most hateful way possible?

Lori thought long and hard about that. Battling her conscience, she rallied her weakening defenses. She couldn't be blamed for reacting the way she had. After all, Noble had kept the truth from her until she fell in love with him. And that just wasn't fair.

Not fair, but you've got it admit it, smart. Real smart. After all, you wouldn't have given him a chance if you'd known.

True.

And so now that you know, you don't love him anymore.

Didn't she wish.

But hey, he's a thief and a murderer, the same sort of lowlife that killed Mick.

"No!" Lori sat upright, her shout filling up the empty room. So empty, so damn empty. Just her, alone with her conscience and a mother lode of hindsight.

The past, the present, the future she had thrown away came into pinpoint focus. Noble hadn't murdered Mick. Noble was not an indiscriminate killer. And as for the robberies, Noble would never take anything that wasn't rightfully his. Lori stared at the empty doorway.

"You screwed up," she whispered. "You really screwed up, lady. The best thing that ever happened in your life is gone because you threw him out. Noble was right—dammit, he was right. His heart *is* pure. He killed purely, he loves just as purely. And that's a helluva lot more than you can say for yourself."

On unsteady legs, she got out of bed and grabbed the wanted poster she'd flung at Noble's face from the floor. Nobody but Noble had any reason to show it to her. How many men would have had the courage, the character and sterling principles it had taken to do such a thing? Only one that she knew of, and now he was gone. All that was left of Noble was a heap of shattered glass, his discarded clothes, and the wanted poster she held.

Lori pressed her lips to the crude likeness of his face.

She ached to kiss him now, tell him that she loved him so much it hurt and that she wanted him back, forever and always.

Lori knew she'd beg him to come back, if that's what he wanted. But first she had to find him. Find him before he—

"Oh God." Suddenly she knew where Noble was going.

"And what about your fears, Noble? What are you afraid of?"

"The lack of your love. Just that. Nothing else."

That's what he'd said, the day before they had gone to his family's burned home, and then the mine. The mine, he was going to the mine! Noble wouldn't care that it was condemned, a death trap. He had no fear of it. He had confronted his only fear.

Lori threw on her clothes, praying he hadn't been able to hitch a ride, praying if he had that he'd still be trying to figure out a way to break in when she got there.

Praying, praying, she raced to the kitchen where she'd left her purse, and rummaged for her keys, then flew to the garage.

Her car was not there.

In its place was a legal pad with a note on it, penned in Noble's script.

To steal a man's horse is a crime worthy of hanging. Hang me if you will for stealing your automobile. I shan't feel the pain of the noose, for you've stolen my very soul. Black as it is, I can't call it an even exchange. You know where I keep my money. Consider it yours. After all, it's a paltry repayment for the many joys you've brought to this dark life of mine. Faithfully, I am yours—Noble

Lori threw down the pad. It landed on a splotch of oil, all that remained of her car.

She had to get some wheels and she had to get them fast. She ran next door, and with grateful eyes she saw that the keys to Mrs. Leaven's sedan were in the ignition, thanks to the elderly lady's trust in her fellowman and her worsening senility.

Lori peeled out the driveway and, once she cleared town, put the pedal to the metal.

The sun was a big orange ball on the horizon when she came to a screeching halt in front of the mine. "Oh no, oh no, oh no," she moaned, leaping from the sedan.

Her own car was half in, half out of the mine. The "Warning Condemned" sign was on the crunched hood, the blockade a mess of splintered wood.

"Noble," she called urgently, her voice echoing down the shaft. Again and again she called him, but only her own voice answered back.

Heart beating fast and furious, she got into her wrecked car and gave thanks that the engine still worked, even though the lights didn't. The laboring sound of the transmission in reverse matched her lung's struggle for air. *God, please, don't let me pass out, I'm not even in there yet.*

She then guided Mrs. Leaven's car to the mine's opening. The sedan's headlights poured into the yawning mouth of the cave.

Lori could feel her hands shaking as she wiped her sweating palms on her thighs and took a determined step forward to face down a fear so severe she was queasy.

She was claustrophobic.

What was that he heard? Something, he'd heard something that wasn't the creak of straining supports. No time to investigate, Noble continued hefting the rocks piled against a nook, placed exactly as he'd left them.

His gold was still there. He could smell it more surely than he smelled the stagnant air that was too dank, too thin from years of closure, making him dangerously light-headed. He had to hurry, take what gold he could carry, and get out.

Another few rocks and—

That sound again. Closer now, it sounded like his name bouncing against the rafters that needed little more than a sneeze to come tumbling down.

A beam creaked overhead, and grainy sprinkles dusted him as he heard a sob and another cry of his name.

Lori. Damn it all to hell, she had no business being here. He had to get her out, quickly, before—

The loud groan of the rafter and a fine mist showering down on him alerted him that he had only minutes, if that long, to grab what gold he could. The first bag was in sight now, he could see it by the light of the lantern he'd brought to work by. Adrenaline pumping, he worked with the speed of a demon, not daring to call to Lori lest she follow him to this place that was about to come apart at the seams.

"Noble!" The sound of a nearby rumble was followed by her scream.

He grabbed the lantern. Oblivious to the bags piled at his feet, he tripped. The lantern flew upward as he instinctively braced his hands for the fall.

The metal hit the giving rafter and he rolled away just before it crashed down claiming the sacks of gold. He could either waste precious seconds pulling them out before the next support gave way—or leave them behind and race as fast as he could to where Lori continued to cry for help.

He left it, every last sack. Without a second's thought, he left the gold and all it represented.

Following the path of her sobs, which blended with the thunder of rock and wood chasing behind him, Noble forced his feet to race faster than his heart. He saw Lori crouched beneath a swaying lantern, debris raining down on her, the beam shifting, starting to fall.

With a lunge, he threw himself against her, knocked her from harm's way, and felt the whoosh of the rafter as it hit the ground, inches from his back. Grabbing her, he longed to berate her for coming after him, to hold her with a savage possession even more. No time, no time for that now. They'd share their future while buried alive if he didn't get them out of there.

"Noble," she panted, holding on to him as he forged ahead and dragged her alongside him. "Noble, thank God—"

"Thank Him once we're safe. Hurry, Lori, faster. *Faster.*"

"But—but my ankle's sprained," she gasped, hobbling, slowing their mad flight. "I twisted it and I couldn't walk and I couldn't catch my breath and—"

"Save your breath." As he swept her up the deadly clamor behind him urged him to surpass his own endurance. Just when Noble was certain his lungs would collapse before his legs did, a thin waft of fresh air sustained him long enough to suck in the next. He knew the cave by heart, knew the entry was still several twists and turns away, knew the mine's destruction was outpacing his flagging speed.

All he had was a hope and a prayer that they'd see another dawn. Together. Whatever their fate, it would be together. In that one realization, Noble found the peace that had eluded him in the span of two lives.

It was with a strange sense of calm that he saw two beacons of light, promising escape and a future of shared dreams.

They escaped just seconds before the final rafter splintered and an explosion of dirt and rocks engulfed the sedan's hood.

Noble sagged to the ground with Lori in his arms, Lori, who was covering his dirty, sweat-streaked face with kisses.

"Now you can thank God," he panted, holding her tighter than tight and vowing never to let her go.

"I do, Noble," she said with a fierce passion. "I thank Him for you. I'm sorry, so sorry for—"

"Hush." He laid a finger to her lips. "All I need to hear is why you came after me."

"Because I love you. Love you, love you, Noble."

The moment he'd heard her call for him, he had known it was true. But still, he was compelled to put Lori's words to a sly test.

"But Lori, I am guilty of a present crime transcending those committed in my past."

Her soft laughter mingled with a sniffle. "They don't hang people for stealing cars. And I'm not pressing charges," she assured him.

"Oh, but the crime I speak of is far more severe. Fortunately, they don't hang people for this one either."

"So tell me, counselor, what is it that you're pleading guilty to?" she asked, holding his face in her hands.

"Why, love, my lady." He kissed her soundly. "Love in the first degree."

"You're guilty, all right," she murmured. "Just as guilty as me." Her gaze alight with this so-called guilt, Lori said solemnly, "So . . . how do you feel about sharing a life sentence together?"

"I'll gladly provide matching nooses. Two bands of gold."

TWENTY

"Look at this, Noble," Lori said excitedly, tapping the medical journal's page. "It says here that 'the most amazing anomaly known to man, who for legal reasons shall remain anonymous, has proven without question that the emerging science of cryonics is not only viable, but an inevitable realization within mankind's grasp.'" She beamed at him, so proud that it was hard not to shout to the world that the anonymous, amazing anomaly was her husband.

"Yes, yes," he muttered. "Quite nice. But, please, love, stop reading aloud. The bar is tomorrow and I need to study. Besides, I care not a whit about what science thinks of me so long as they remember I shall trample them in court should my identity be made known and our privacy invaded."

"But, Noble," she persisted, "because of you, the government's funneling in tons of dollars for research. Think of all the people who'll have a second chance at life. Maybe even people like you and me. I mean, wouldn't it be great if we could get frozen together and come back in a hundred years, maybe hang out in that century until we got tired of it, then decide which one we wanted to check out next?"

"I am quite happy living out the rest of our years in this century, thank you." Noble snatched the medical journal and flung it away. "I'm also quite happy to spend them here in our new home. Not as grand as what I wished to give you and our children, but as my practice grows we'll build on. Hopefully, some of the land will still be available and we can purchase a good parcel of it."

"Even if it's gone, at least we have the acreage we really wanted. I'm sure your parents would be pleased to know that our foundation is where theirs used to be."

"In more ways than one." Noble linked his hand with hers. "Love, the strongest foundation of all. Neither time nor death can weaken its hold." And then he whispered something against her belly. No doubt a word of love and a gentle warning to their unborn child to stay quiet, just as he would in future years when he recounted the adventures of his ancestor whose name and likeness on a wanted poster he was given the honor to inherit.

Eyeing the stack of papers between them, Lori smiled suggestively. "I thought you had a bar exam to study for."

Noble tapped his lips. "Never mind that now," he said briskly. "After all, if I could secure a birth certificate and recent diploma in exchange for my contribution to science, if I could father a child despite the primitive freezing and thawing of my seed, if I could demand and get an order prohibiting any future contact with me, my wife, and any number of children we might have . . . Ah well, given all that, passing the bar, almost prepared, should prove an easy enough task."

"Why Noble Zhivago, barrister, I daresay you're a pistol," she quipped, imitating his most proper British accent.

He chuckled and tossed his legal pads and law books to the floor. After a soft kiss, he carefully settled himself on top of her and proudly said, "And you, my lady, have me in your pocket."

THE EDITOR'S CORNER

Spring is on its way, and with it come four wonderful new LOVESWEPTs. You'll want to lose yourself in these terrific stories with funny, interesting and sexy characters written by some of the most talented authors writing women's fiction today.

Starting things off is the ever-popular Charlotte Hughes with **HUSBAND WANTED**, LOVESWEPT #734. Fannie Brisbane knows it is an impossible scheme, but unless she agrees to it, the daughter she gave up for adoption years ago will know the truth, that she's not rich and married! Her Griddle and Grill customers all pitch in, offering clothes, even a mansion—but when Clay Bodine offers to play her husband, Fannie doesn't know if she should dare say yes to a charade with the man who's always owned her heart. With her trademark humor and unforgettable characters, Charlotte delivers another sweetly sizzling romance that resonates with tenderness and sparkles with fun.

Linda Cajio's heroine has found **THE PERFECT CATCH**, LOVESWEPT #735. Elaine Sampson cheers joyfully, waving her arms as the player rounds the bases—and drenches the gorgeous guy in front of her with ice and cola! Graham Reed accepts her apology, but when the pretty teacher follows him to the men's room to help clean his suit, he laughs . . . and wonders if he is falling in love. He makes her reckless, kisses her senseless, but this handsome hunk might be a little out of her league. Linda's delightful love story hits an out-of-the-park home run!

Welcome Faye Hughes, a wonderfully talented new writer debuting at Loveswept with **CAN'T FIGHT THE FEELING**, LOVESWEPT #736. It took Justin Stone five minutes to fall in love with Morgan Tremayne—and nearly six years to recover from their quickie divorce ten months later! Now Morgan is back—flirting, teasing, igniting desires that have never really died—and determined to show her beloved pirate that she is his destiny. Once he wooed her with poetry and kisses that melted her clothes off, but now he wants to claim his fallen angel at last. Wildly sexy and delightfully outrageous, this sensational novel by Faye will enchant readers with a story that's as playful as it is seductive.

Last but not least is the fabulous Linda Warren with **AFTER MIDNIGHT**, LOVESWEPT #737. Cord Prescott never asks if Arianna Rossini is guilty when he comes to bail her out of jail, but something unspoken passes between them and tells him she didn't embezzle the missing money. But when she asks for a deal instead of a trial, he aches to learn her secrets, to persuade her to surrender the truth. Consumed by desire, haunted by guilt, Ari must help Cord make peace with his own demons. In a novel that's all at once provocative, passionate, and poignant, Linda explores a forbidden love between a rebel attorney who's won everything but a woman's heart and a lady whose mystery may be innocence or deceit.

Happy reading!

With warmest wishes,

Beth de Guzman

Shauna Summers

Beth de Guzman   Shauna Summers
Senior Editor   Assistant Editor

P.S. Don't miss the women's novels coming your way in April: **MISTRESS,** by Amanda Quick, is the terrific *New York Times* bestseller, in paperback for the first time; **DANGEROUS TO KISS,** by the award-winning Elizabeth Thornton, is an unforgettable historical romance in the tradition of Amanda Quick and Jane Feather, set in Regency England; **LONG NIGHT MOON,** by highly acclaimed author

Theresa Weir, is a gripping and emotional romance in which a brash reporter helps an ethereal beauty escape a harrowing life. And immediately following this page, look for a preview of the exciting romances from Bantam that are *available now!*

Don't miss these fantastic books
by your favorite Bantam authors

On sale in February:

NIGHT SINS
by Tami Hoag

THE FOREVER TREE
by Rosanne Bittner

**MY GUARDIAN ANGEL
ANTHOLOGY**
by Kay Hooper
Sandra Chastain
Susan Krinard
Karyn Monk
Elizabeth Thornton

PAGAN BRIDE
by Tamara Leigh

"A master of the genre."
—*Publishers Weekly*

NIGHT SINS

by

TAMI HOAG

Available in Hardcover

Every once in a while a thriller comes along that stretches the limits of the genre and takes readers places they have never been before. Night Sins *is such a novel. . . .*

Deer Lake is a small Minnesota town where people know their neighbors and crime is something that happens on the evening news. But the illusion of safety is shattered when eight-year-old Josh Kirkwood disappears from a hockey rink as he waits for his mother to pick him up after practice. The only thing the police find is his duffel bag with a note stuffed inside: ignorance is not innocence but SIN.

The following is a chilling preview of what transpires the night Hannah realizes her son is missing.

"I forgot. I forgot he was waiting."
A fresh wave of tears washed down Hannah's

cheeks and fell like raindrops onto the lap of her long wool skirt. She doubled over, wanting to curl into a ball while the emotions tore at her. Mitch leaned closer and stroked her hair, trying to offer some comfort. The cop in him remained calm, waiting for facts, reciting the likely explanations. Deeper inside, the parent in him experienced a sharp stab of instinctive fear.

"When I g-got to the rink he w-was g-gone."

"Well, honey, Paul probably picked him up—"

"No. Wednesday is *my* night."

"Did you call Paul to check?"

"I tried, but he wasn't in the office."

"Then Josh probably got a ride with one of the other kids. He's probably at some buddy's house—"

"No. I called everyone I could think of. I checked at the sitter's—Sue Bartz. I thought maybe he would be there waiting for me to come pick up Lily, but Sue hadn't seen him." And Lily was still there waiting for her mother, probably wondering why mama had come and gone without her. "I checked at home, just in case he decided to walk. I called the other hockey moms. I drove back to the rink. I drove back to the hospital. *I can't find him.*"

"Do you have a picture of your son?" Megan asked as she came around the desk.

"His school picture. It's not the best—he needed a haircut, but there wasn't time." Hannah pulled her purse up onto her lap. Her hands shook as she dug through the leather bag for her wallet. "He brought the slip home from school and I made a note, but then time just got away from me and I— forgot."

She whispered the last word as she opened to the

photograph of Josh. *I forgot.* Such a simple, harmless excuse. Forgot about his picture. Forgot about his haircut. Forgot him. Her hand trembled so badly she could barely manage to slip the photograph from the plastic window. She offered it to the dark-haired woman, realizing belatedly that she had no idea who the woman was.

"I'm sorry," she murmured, dredging up the ingrained manners and a fragile smile. "Have we met?"

Mitch sat back against the edge of the desk again. "I'm sorry, Hannah. This is Agent O'Malley with the Bureau of Criminal Apprehension. Megan, this is Dr. Hannah Garrison, head of the emergency room in our community hospital. One of the best doctors ever to wield a stethoscope," he added with a ghost of a grin. "We're very lucky to have her."

Megan studied the photograph, her mind on business, not social niceties. A boy of eight or nine wearing a Cub Scout uniform stared out at her. He had a big gap-toothed grin and a smattering of freckles across his nose and cheeks. His hair was an unruly mop of sandy brown curls. His blue eyes were brimming with life and mischief.

"Is he normally a pretty responsible boy?" Megan asked. "Does he know to call you if he's going to be late or to get permission to go to a friend's house?"

Hannah nodded. "Josh is very levelheaded."

"What did he wear to school today?"

Hannah rubbed a hand across her forehead, trying to think back to morning. It seemed as much a dream as any of this, long ago and foggy. Lily crying at the indignity of being confined to her high chair. Josh skating around the kitchen floor in his stocking feet. Permission slip needed signing for a field trip to the Science Museum. Homework done? Spelling words memorized? A call from the hospital. French toast burning on the stove. Paul storming around the kitchen, snapping at Josh, complaining about the shirts that needed ironing.

"Um—jeans. A blue sweater. Snow boots. A ski jacket—bright blue with bright yellow and bright green trim. Um . . . his Viking stocking cap—it's yellow with a patch sewn on. Paul wouldn't let him wear a purple one with that wild coat. He said it would look like Josh was dressed by color-blind gypsies. I couldn't see the harm; he's only eight years old . . ."

Megan handed the photograph back and looked up at Mitch. "I'll call it in right away." Her mind was already on the possibilities and the steps they should take in accordance with those possibilities. "Get the bulletin to your people, the sheriff's department, the highway patrol—"

Hannah looked stricken. "You don't think—"

"No," Mitch interceded smoothly. "No, honey, of course not. It's just standard procedure. We'll put out a bulletin to all the guys on patrol so if they see Josh they'll know to pick him up and bring him home.

"Excuse us for just a minute," he said, holding up a finger. He turned his back to Hannah and a furious look to Megan. "I need to give Agent O'Malley a few instructions."

He clamped a hand on Megan's shoulder and herded her unceremoniously out the door and into the narrow, dimly-lit hall. A round-headed man in a tweed blazer and chinos gave them a dirty look and stuck a finger in his free ear as he tried to have a conversation on a pay phone outside the men's room door. Mitch hit the phone's plunger with two fingers, cutting off the conversation and drawing an indignant "Hey!" from the caller.

"Excuse us," Mitch growled, flashing his badge. "Police business."

He shouldered the man away from the phone and sent him hustling down the hall with a scowl that had scattered petty drug pushers and hookers from the meanest streets in Miami. He turned the same scowl on Megan. He towered over her and had to outweigh her by a good eighty pounds. He had physically intimidated men who were twice her size and mean as alligators. Yet she glared right back at him.

"What the hell is wrong with you?" she snapped, jumping on the offensive, knowing it was her best defense. She could feel his temper, a physical heat that seared her skin.

"What the hell is wrong with me?" Mitch barked, keeping his voice low. "What the hell is wrong with you—scaring the poor woman—"

"She has reason to be scared, Chief. Her son is missing."

"That has yet to be established. He's probably playing at a friend's house."

"She says she checked with his friends."

"Yes, but she's panicked. She's probably forgotten to look in an obvious place."

"Or somebody grabbed the kid."

Mitch scowled harder because it took an effort to

dismiss her suggestion outright. "This is Deer Lake, O'Malley, not New York."

Megan arched a brow. "You don't have crime in Deer Lake? You have a police force. You have a jail. Or is that all just window dressing?"

"Of course we have crime," he snarled. "We have college students who shoplift and cheese factory workers who get drunk on Saturday night and try to beat each other up in the American Legion parking lot. We don't have child abductions, for Christ's sake."

"Yeah, well, welcome to the nineties, Chief," she said sarcastically. "It can happen anywhere."

"Power, passion, tragedy, and triumph are Rosanne Bittner's hallmarks. Again and again, she brings readers to tears."
—*Romantic Times*

THE FOREVER TREE
by
Rosanne Bittner

Against the glorious, golden land of California, award-winning Rosanne Bittner creates another sweeping saga of passion, tragedy, and adventure . . . as a Spanish beauty and a rugged New Englander struggle against all odds to carve out an empire—and to forge a magnificent love.

Here is a look at this powerful novel.

Señorita Lopez, what are you doing here alone?"

"I often come here," Santana answered. "*Mi padre* lets me go riding alone, as long as it is only to this place that he knows I love." She looked up at the lone pine tree. "I hope that you would never cut this tree, or those around it that protect and shelter it. I feel sorry for it. It seems so alone here, so I come to keep it company. I call it my forever tree."

"The forever tree. Why is that?"

She shrugged. "When I think about how old the California pines become, and how young this one still is, I know it will be here for a very long time, long after I die, even though I am only sixteen." Will saw a shadow of sadness cross her face. "So many things in life change as we grow older, but a tree is forever, a sign that some things never have to change."

He frowned, touched by the way she described the tree as something with a heart and soul. That was how he felt about trees himself, that they were a form of living poetry, something strong yet warm, something that gave so many things to man—shade, homes, paper, the warmth of a wood fire . . . "I'm glad to know you love trees as much as I do," he answered. He was sure he was not supposed to be alone with her this way, but he didn't care. She wore no veil, no special jewelry. Like the day she had come to his room, she was simply dressed. She needed nothing to add to her beauty.

"I love trees very much, *señor*, and the birds, the animals . . ."

Will smiled. "I wish you would just call me Will."

Santana felt a flush coming to her cheeks. "It is best that I do not," she said, smiling shyly. "Well, perhaps whenever I see you alone this way."

Will wondered if that meant she wanted to meet alone with him more often. That did not seem wise, but then, she was too young to be wise, and he was too enamored with her when she was near like this to care about doing the wise thing himself. "Good," he answered. "I have enjoyed getting to know you and your family, Santana. May I call you Santana?"

"*Si*, when we are alone."

Will looked her over, thinking how lovely her naked body must be under her dark riding habit. "I doubt that will happen very often."

She shrugged. "I suppose not. You will be very busy soon with building your mill, and I will be busy with my schooling, and with preparing myself for marriage."

He caught the bitterness in her words. "Surely you don't really want to marry Hugo Bolivar."

She turned away. "That is a forbidden subject."

Will sighed. "All right then, what *can* we talk about?" A little voice warned him that he should get on his horse and ride hell-bent out of there. A stronger force, though, made him stay. For more than two weeks now he had argued with himself that he should keep out of this woman's business, but every time he saw her at meals, listened to her talk, realized what a lovely and innocent woman-child she was, he felt anger and frustration at the thought of her becoming Hugo's wife.

Their eyes met. "*Gracias*," she said. "You are a very nice man, Will Lassater. I like talking with you. You make it easy. I can never find anything to talk about with Hugo. He only likes to talk about himself and his riches." She looked away, realizing she had said something she had not meant to say. "I suppose I will get used to him. Once he is my husband, we will have many things to talk about, and there will be children to share."

A pain stabbed through Will's gut at the thought

of Bolivar bedding Santana. He had no doubt the man would be rough and demanding. "You don't really want to marry that man and have children by him, do you?"

Santana rose, walking a few feet away. "I told you I cannot talk about that. I should not have even mentioned him."

"Nobody knows we're talking about it. Something tells me you *need* to talk about it, Santana. Probably nobody else you know understands how much you detest marrying Hugo. They all think you should be honored and privileged to marry such a man. But you don't want to, do you?"

MY GUARDIAN ANGEL

Five bewitching tales of romance from
**Sandra Chastain   Kay Hooper
Susan Krinard   Karyn Monk
Elizabeth Thornton**

ALMOST AN ANGEL by Kay Hooper
A handsome British agent won't rest until he finds the beautiful stranger who miraculously rescued him—then vanished as quickly as she appeared.

GUARDIAN OF THE HEART by Sandra Chastain
A brave young widow is left alone to fend for herself on the banks of the Rio Grande, until the ghost of her husband brings her a second chance at love.

ANGEL ON MY SHOULDER by Susan Krinard
A lovely actress torn from her lover's arms finds that her beloved pet, a wily parrot, houses a spirit determined to see that the two meet again.

SAVING CELESTE by Karyn Monk
A Bostonian with a tragic past prevents a despairing young woman from throwing herself off a bridge, and discovers that she holds the key to his happiness.

THE TROUBLE WITH ANGELS
by Elizabeth Thornton
The rakish young footman from Dangerous to Love makes a reappearance, this time dancing attendance on a spoiled beauty bent on landing a titled husband. It's all Flynn can do to keep his charge's reputation intact—and his hands to himself.

"Fresh, exciting . . . wonderfully sensual
. . . sure to be noticed in the romance
genre."
—Amanda Quick

PAGAN BRIDE
by
Tamara Leigh

*Bound by the chains of slavery in an exotic land, Lucien de
Gautier had only one chance of escape. In exchange for his
freedom, he pledged to smuggle a virtuous young woman
out of a harem and onto a ship bound for England. But
Lucien couldn't know that the real danger would lie not in
the long voyage ahead, but in his dazzling charge: a ravishing innocent whose flame-red hair and emerald eyes
would unleash his most potent desires. . . .*

The music grew louder, its vigorous beat coursing
through every vein in every limb that moved to it.
Tightly, it wound itself around the slender woman
who swayed at the center of the large room. It pulled
her head back and closed her eyes against the light. It
drew her arms up from her sides and spread them
wide to embrace the sensual rhythm she had given
herself over to. It shook her shoulders, rotated

and jerked her hips, and caused her fingers to snap.

The female dancers who had been hired to entertain the women of Abd al-Jabbar's harem drifted away, going to stand along the walls and watch this strange one who had joined in the dance.

She was different from the other women, her hair a flame amid the ashes. Skin that should have been pale was tanned and faintly touched with freckles. Though fine-boned and slim, her body curved where it ought to, her breasts full and firm. And those pale green eyes—they were full of daring and laughter when she turned them upon her captive audience.

All watched as the tempo quickened and the solitary dancer swept across the floor, sparkling laughter spilling from her throat as the music pulled her deeper into its spell.

Unmindful of the pins holding her veil in place, the young woman snatched the translucent material from her waist-length hair and drew it taut between her hands. Then, raising her arms above her head, she pivoted on the balls of her bare feet. Faster and faster she turned, until she whirled in the wake of the diaphanous material clothing her limbs.

More laughter parted her lips, followed by a shriek of delight as the music reached its zenith. She was lost in it—completely given over to its control.

"Alessandra!" A reproving voice split the air.

The music fell away, and a din of women's voices rose to take its place.

Wrenched from the trancelike state she had slipped into, Alessandra staggered around to face her mother's displeasure. However, the room continued to revolve as if she were still dancing.

She sank to her knees and sat back on her heels, the dizziness making it impossible for her to focus on the woman who stood at the far end of the room.

Standing betwen Sabine and Khalid, Lucien knew he was in trouble. He had known the moment Sabine had called out to the wild dancer, naming her the one. Inwardly, he groaned and cursed his man's flesh. One look at the young woman as she whirled across the floor was all it had taken to decide him. Thinking her a dancer—though with her mother's hair falling down her back, he should have known otherwise—he had determined to have her as soon as possible. Then the accursed woman at his side had shattered the possibility. Or had she?

And don't miss these outstanding romances from Bantam Books, on sale in March:

MISTRESS
Available in paperback
by the *New York Times* bestselling author
Amanda Quick
"Amanda Quick is one of the most versatile and talented authors of the decade."
—*Romantic Times*

DANGEROUS TO KISS
by the award-winning
Elizabeth Thornton
"A major, major talent . . . a superstar."
—*Romantic Times*

LONG NIGHT MOON
by the incomparable
Theresa Weir
"Theresa Weir's writing is poignant, passionate and powerful."
—Jayne Ann Krentz

*To enter the sweepstakes outlined below, you must respond by the date specified and
follow all entry instructions published elsewhere in this offer.*

DREAM COME TRUE SWEEPSTAKES

Sweepstakes begins 9/1/94, ends 1/15/96. To qualify for the Early Bird Prize, entry must be received by the date specified elsewhere in this offer. Winners will be selected in random drawings on 2/29/96 by an independent judging organization whose decisions are final. Early Bird winner will be selected in a separate drawing from among all qualifying entries.

Odds of winning determined by total number of entries received. Distribution not to exceed 300 million.

Estimated maximum retail value of prizes: Grand (1) $25,000 (cash alternative $20,000); First (1) $2,000; Second (1) $750; Third (50) $75; Fourth (1,000) $50; Early Bird (1) $5,000. Total prize value: $86,500.

Automobile and travel trailer must be picked up at a local dealer; all other merchandise prizes will be shipped to winners. Awarding of any prize to a minor will require written permission of parent/guardian. If a trip prize is won by a minor, s/he must be accompanied by parent/legal guardian. Trip prizes subject to availability and must be completed within 12 months of date awarded. Blackout dates may apply. Early Bird trip is on a space available basis and does not include port charges, gratuities, optional shore excursions and onboard personal purchases. Prizes are not transferable or redeemable for cash except as specified. No substitution for prizes except as necessary due to unavailability. Travel trailer and/or automobile license and registration fees are winners' responsibility as are any other incidental expenses not specified herein.

Early Bird Prize may not be offered in some presentations of this sweepstakes. Grand through third prize winners will have the option of selecting any prize offered at level won. All prizes will be awarded. Drawing will be held at 204 Center Square Road, Bridgeport, NJ 08014. Winners need not be present. For winners list (available in June, 1996), send a self-addressed, stamped envelope by 1/15/96 to: Dream Come True Winners, P.O. Box 572, Gibbstown, NJ 08027.

THE FOLLOWING APPLIES TO THE SWEEPSTAKES ABOVE:

No purchase necessary. No photocopied or mechanically reproduced entries will be accepted. Not responsible for lost, late, misdirected, damaged, incomplete, illegible, or postage-die mail. Entries become the property of sponsors and will not be returned.

Winner(s) will be notified by mail. Winner(s) may be required to sign and return an affidavit of eligibility/release within 14 days of date on notification or an alternate may be selected. Except where prohibited by law, entry constitutes permission to use of winners' names, hometowns, and likenesses for publicity without additional compensation. Void where prohibited or restricted. All federal, state, provincial, and local laws and regulations apply.

All prize values are in U.S. currency. Presentation of prizes may vary; values at a given prize level will be approximately the same. All taxes are winners' responsibility.

Canadian residents, in order to win, must first correctly answer a time-limited skill testing question administered by mail. Any litigation regarding the conduct and awarding of a prize in this publicity contest by a resident of the province of Quebec may be submitted to the Regie des loteries et courses du Quebec.

Sweepstakes is open to legal residents of the U.S., Canada, and Europe (in those areas where made available) who have received this offer.

Sweepstakes in sponsored by Ventura Associates, 1211 Avenue of the Americas, New York, NY 10036 and presented by independent businesses. Employees of these, their advertising agencies and promotional companies involved in this promotion, and their immediate families, agents, successors, and assignees shall be ineligible to participate in the promotion and shall not be eligible for any prizes covered herein. SWP 3/95